ADAM SANTO
TEMPERATURE: DEAD + RISING

ADAM SANTO

Copyright © 2010 Adam Santo

All rights reserved.

ISBN: 145365853X
ISBN-13: 9781453658536

LCCN: 2010909583

DEDICATION

This book is dedicated to my son, Mitchell. May he continue a love for reading and one write himself.

ACKNOWLEDGMENTS

A thank you goes to all of my family for enduring the countless hours of typing late into the night.

CHAPTER 1

The figure moved to a side entrance looking for the security pad that employees used to open the door, hidden within darkened spaces where security lights did not reach. Moonlight reflected off the newly formed frost, making the grass a star-scape on the ground. The fragile ice crystals crunched underfoot as a cloaked figure approached under the building's deep shadows. A quick glance gave the intruder satisfaction for solitude while he swiped the fake ID across a glowing panel access. He grunted dispassionately after the dull, buzzing red light from the panel denied him entrance. He should have updated the card through one of his contacts before he tried tonight. He pocketed the badge as he leaned down near the pad to whisper a few words.

His words made the air draw inward to the panel causing small violet sparks to bounce along its exterior. To his relief the pad chimed back showing a green light and a click of the inner lock. He slipped in through the partially open door after a quick look to check for any passing staff around the immediate vicinity within the building. The figure stripped off his trench coat revealing a pristine white coat underneath, retrieving the pocketed badge to pin on the coat's pocket. With the trench coat over his arm, he made his way to the bay of elevators pressing the down button. Portraying a doctor should buy some time for him to reach his mark and make it back out before suspicion arose.

He entered the elevator with a female quick on his heels. She impatiently pressed the button for an upper floor, and he automatically pressed the one above it so he would not get off too soon. To his relief she only looked him over once before ignoring him on the ride up. He was just fine with that.

After she exited the elevator, he immediately pressed the button for one of the bottom floors. He was not here to see anyone living at this time. There was not anyone left in his life that could be alive to care for anymore. The short distraction of riding up one more floor before making it to the lower levels might have cost him precious time he could not waste; the ritual was going to happen soon.

Just before the elevator doors opened, he whispered a chant of undecipherable words that caused the air around him to quake and vibrate violently. As fast as it had started, the air went still, leaving behind a faint shimmer of confetti slowly falling to the floor. The elevator doors opened as he walked through the suspended curtain of sparkling light.

The figure who left the doors behind was not the person who had entered it earlier any longer. He no longer stood 5'11" with brown, shoulder-length hair and a light tan. He now had short hair with blond highlights, stood two inches taller, and sported a deeper tan. Quickly glancing at the mounted wall plaque showed the different departments on this level; giving him the directions he needed to reach his destination; the morgue.

Flickering from the overhead fluorescent lights caused him concern, but it might've just been some bulbs that needed replacing. "Nothing to worry about," he muttered. Lost in mapping out the getaway route in his head, he followed the intermittent signs placed on walls to show the way, abruptly coming to a hallway leading for the morgue.

A cursory inspection of this hallway and various rooms near the morgue he had passed proved empty. Three remaining hallways branched off from the one he was in. It was his duty to check for anyone still in the area and clear them out safely and without raising suspicion. It was his priority before the ritual started.

Too late.

Lights overhead flickered faster than a shutterbug's worst nightmare, giving way to some of the fluorescent bulbs bursting randomly. He picked up his pace as he checked the first branching hallway only to be relieved that it was empty. When he turned to continue the search for wandering workers, more bulbs burst, leaving ballast covers to break away and creating a rain of broken glass shards to scatter across the floor. Bolts of brightening light preceded each bulb's explosion as he ran for the next hallway trying to steer away from falling debris in the process. Clearing the second of three hallways was not going to be an issue with light fixtures exploding the way they were. That should drive off any loose groups of people in a hurry.

Bursting through the morgue doors would be futile and deadly at this point, as he saw the flashes of light solidify into ghostly orbs and float to what could only be the ritual's center. The ritual was older than time itself, requiring no one to be present for it to be completed. All he could do was sit and wait until it was over. He could not get any closer than he already was or he would perish by the powerful magic at work. This ritual, called the Wakening, drew in every bit of living essence relating to life in order to complete the final stages. In this windowless space below the hospital, an absence of light became profound. Even emergency lights did not turn on after everything else went dark in the immediate area. Orbs of brilliant light formed from points along the hallway where blasts from the light bulbs tore away flimsy metal fixtures. The exposed wiring produced sparks from overhead fixtures, providing only flashes of illumination and subdued lighting in an otherwise pitch black atmosphere.

There was a tangible pull nagging at him from the morgue's interior as distant balls of ghostly light still trailed down branching hallways to their destination leaving streamers of fading light in their wake. Those same orbs stopped in midflight to hover in the air, indicating a climax of what was about to happen behind closed doors. Crackling emanated from the closest ball of light as it grew in intensity and the air around him grew thick. He knew what was coming next, but the only thing left to do was protect himself from the final stage of the ritual. Out of time and nowhere to turn for safety, he chanted a protective shield into place, finishing the last word of incantation just as orbs were forced from the morgue in the opposite direction of the door.

His body did not normally feel subtle changes in temperature around him, but in this case he felt them from the inside, like something cooking in a microwave. The translucent oval shield could hold out against anything physically thrown at it for a short time, however, he doubted it would hold up to the Wakening's powers. He became hot, the sensation beginning in his core and working its way out. The paint on the walls bubbled, small bubbles at first then growing in size. A blast of heat from beyond the doors raced out, blowing with such force that one of the hinges broke free from the doorjamb on its way out. The light sucked in moments before had turned into pure heat, causing the blast from the inner sanctum of the morgue to be bigger than it should have been—one of the reasons this ritual was usually done outdoors in an open field. His mark had not been found in time to move him or her outdoors. Trailing black scorch marks on the walls were left behind from the unstoppable force blowing free of its confines. Dust from what could have been the remains of paperwork settled in the wake of the ritual's remarkable display, and then all went quiet.

It was over; the whole thing might have lasted fifteen minutes, but it felt behind such devastation. Now all he had to do was find the mark, convince the person to come with him, and get out unseen. Emergency lights had kicked on during the aftermath of the ritual.

A little too late, he smirked as the thought rolled around his head.

They illuminated the hallways in pools of glowing light, leaving spaces in between the soft pools of light on the floor darker than they should have been. Distracted by a show of force that the ritual preformed, he had not noticed it leeching away his own magical disguise in the process. His useless shield had dissolved with it. The tugging urgency he felt within him brought the stranger's mind back to task. Not concerned with the apparent loss, he focused more on his ultimate goal. He only had a few yards to go before entering the morgue proper.

Pushing past the disheveled and broken doors, he found rows of stainless steel doors with cold storage drawers lining the wall. Residue from the ritual still lingered on one of the doors to his target's tomb-like resting place, almost appearing to drip from the door. A voice began to get louder from behind the stainless steel door as he pulled a magnetized clipboard off the door in search of a name for the person within. Her name was Sally Mertill. He reached for the door's handle to release her. A single latch securing the door broke free sending him flying through the air from the impact. Sally thrust out with her hands against the back wall of her confines, a raw cry spewing forth from her throat before closing her in again.

Her outcry grew in intensity after the door swung open once more, bouncing back once off its hinges to resonate like a gong. Sprawled on the floor from the impact and concerned someone might have heard her, he bounded to his feet, back to the partially opened cubicle. Her exertion from the screaming and flailing about had left her apparently spent with only enough energy to shiver in place, letting the white sheet, fitted specifically for the drawer space, fall free unnoticed.

"I'm here to help," he whispered to her, hoping she was coherent enough to acknowledge him.

He walked away finding something more suitable to cover her nakedness as she replied, "C-c-cold."

He saw her prop up on elbows with an effort to survey her surroundings, taking it all in with a slow resolve. Surprise and concern were visibly the emotions of the moment as she took it all in. Although he could tell she was beginning to understand what the room signified, she still asked with a shaky voice, "Where are we and who are you?"

He felt time slipping away; soon someone would enter, and answering her questions could prevent them from moving quickly. He retrieved a larger white sheet, tossed it to her, and turned around to give some semblance of privacy while he talked.

"To keep this simple, my name is Bocnic. For the rest of your query, I'm afraid there isn't much time to cover it all just now." He turned when she cleared her throat, giving him the cue it was all right to turn back to face her. "Now, if we can get moving I will have plenty to share once we are free of this place, but if you want to stay and find out why these people put you in that drawer, then by all means stay and find out."

He waited tensely for her to answer as she took another look around, surely conflicted about making such a choice so quickly. When she took a step in his direction, he took it as a good sign she would come with him. He glanced approvingly one last time at the way she used her sheet to cover up before leading the way to the exit.

The emergency lights did not broadcast far enough to show the damaged doors clearly and Sally spoke up. "You had to break in to get me?" she asked, shock filling her words.

The honest answer was yes; keeping it from being a complete lie. "I had to break in to find you," Bocnic said, listening for any footsteps down the hall.

He did not like to lie, much; and he did not intend to start off their first encounter that way. But Sally might change her mind about him helping her if see sensed something wrong with his words. Using the broken doors she evidently took his answer to mean gave credence to his little white lie of how he really got in. Whatever kept her moving forward worked for him.

Passing through the dislodged doorway brought them into the main hallway. Bocnic guided Sally to the first hallway branch he had hid in earlier. It took them passed a set of elevators closer to the main entrance of the hospital than where he came in. There was no traffic coming from the distance. They could see the brilliant shine of light ahead reflecting off polished floors beyond the cascade of emergency lighting. Showing where the Wakening's reach stopped and life carried on. Voices could be heard in the distance, signaling a need for stealth, when Sally inexcusably sneezed. Bocnic hoped the sudden noise did not bring someone their way to investigate. He shushed her as they made their way down the shortening hallway to the next branch of the journey and closer to the noises ahead.

The closer they got, more sounds became clear as moans, groans, and the expected sounds of pain filtered through the nurses rambling about the abrupt blackout. They ducked into one of the doors closest to the corner, giving Bocnic time to think. There had been more accidents in the past week than the hospital could handle, causing them to set up temporary ICU care centers on multiple floors to compensate for the overflow of patients. How many people were now hurt or dead because of Sally's resurrection? Too many, from what he saw; the Wakening had never caused this much damage in the past. A few deaths were common surrounding a Wakening, but this many could not be mere coincidence.

As the door closed behind them, they could hear more voices echoing down the darkened hallways discussing the blown light bulbs and how a power surge could have done all the damage. Bocnic suggested they sit tight while people down the hall cleared out before moving on. Sally, still terrified to do much more, did as she was told. So much had happened in so short a time that Bocnic could see she felt more than just a little confused at the moment.

Once the footsteps began to fade in the direction of the makeshift ICU counter, Bocnic ushered her out to the hallway once more before she got the nerve up to ask any questions. Her face had drawn up in that inquisitive demeanor that he had seen on past newly risen. Standing by the corner allowed him a clear view of the elevators and keeping her from speaking by avoiding her eyes; all they had to do was wait. Someone would either need to go upstairs or exit the elevator sooner or later. They did not have to wait long.

A maintenance man had been called to assess the damage before any repairs could be done as he had hoped. While everyone was busy at the reception desk, Bocnic took advantage of the situation and headed for the open elevator's doors, making it safely into the awaiting cabin as the doors noiselessly closed.

In the quiet of the elevator and looking a bit more defrosted from the brisk walking they had undertaken, Sally turned to her savior, Bocnic kidded himself with the thought, not sure if that was what he was yet to her and said, "What is going on?"

"It's still too soon and we are not yet in the clear. Could you give us time enough to breathe fresh outdoor air before we get into that?" Bocnic felt his voice sounded a little rougher than it should have been, but he could not lose the momentum they had gained.

Sally stood glaring at him for a moment before she spoke again. "We have less than a minute until the doors open, so you need to tell me something more or I won't keep following you. Besides the fact that you're getting me out of a very cold situation, I can't see following you blindly the rest of the way. Give me more or I walk."

"OK. Staying here will get you killed or worse."

She made to interrupt him but he held up his hand for patience. "We have little time to discuss why you woke up in cold storage, but the people that put you there expect to find the drawer still occupied."

The ding of the elevator drew their attention to the cabin's doors as they silently opened. Bocnic glanced around for trouble in the immediate vicinity before leading the way out. "You coming?"

CHAPTER 2

He'd just walked away!

Is he that confident about me to think I would not turn away and seek out a cop or anyone for that matter? Does he really think that explanation was enough to convince me into following? So many unanswered questions swam through Sally's head as she stood watching Bocnic make his way past the reception desk for the front doors beyond. The elevator doors began closing, making her reach a hand out to stop them. Before she knew it, she stood facing a wall outside the elevator shaft glaring at a clock above: it read 4:23 a.m. Her thoughts raced as she tried to decide what to do. The next shift would be coming in soon to relieve the night crew, and the thought made her skin crawl. She doubted Bocnic had lied to her about what might happen below the hospital's main floors if she stayed.

By the time Sally made up her mind to follow this so-called rescuer, he had already left the building. She checked her makeshift wrap one more time, noticing it dragged on the ground, which could hamper her impending escape. Hiking up the make-believe hem, she walked at a fast pace to her goal. The reception area was designed to be an open space with area rug carpets instead of walls in honor of Colorado's motto to the Open Spaces Project. This was convenient for her as she cut through between chairs and end tables to reach the front doors. Sally was halfway to the automatic glass doors when the nurse behind the front desk called out to her.

"Mrs.?" The nurse cautiously spoke at first. When Sally did not turn around the nurse became persistent.

She ignored the nurse's insistence that she come to the front desk, and picked up her pace toward freedom. The nurse came around the desk to follow her out, but Sally picked it up to a trot. At the automated doors, Sally glanced back at her pursuer while the doors took their time to slowly open. The nurse had returned to the desk with the phone receiver at her ear apparently calling security. Sally hurried out into the cold world waiting beyond.

A bitterly cold fall wind ripped through the thin bedsheet, causing goose bumps to ring out along her body from head to toe. She shivered as she took a moment to find which way Bocnic went. A car pulled up to the curb's loading/unloading zone in the roundabout driveway twenty yards away, flashing headlights. Bocnic emerged from the driver's side and waved at her to get in. Noise from the other side of the glass doors made her turn around to see security guards heading her direction. Spurred again by indecision and fear, she galloped over to the waiting car as he dropped back into the driver's seat. He pulled the latch for the passenger's side door to have it swing open right when she reached the car. Closing the door behind her with a little help of the car accelerating away from the hospital startled her as they sped off.

Sally noticed he was heading north when she gained her bearing, taking in the sights from almost deserted streets of Colorado Springs through amber pools of light left behind by streetlights. Bocnic did not seem to be in much of a hurry as they meandered down side street after side street, but always heading north. She needed to gather her thoughts before saying anything rash, and the only way she knew how was through music. Flipping the dial around until she found her favorite rock station kept her from thinking too hard about anything. The song blaring out was one from Nonpoint singing "What a Day," bringing out a giggle then a laugh from her. *More like "What a Night,* she thought as she tried to stifle the laugh altogether when Bocnic looked her way questioningly. The sudden outburst put her in a better frame of mind to think about questions for this so-called savior. Not that he claimed the title.

She started with the simplest and would work her way up from there, "Who are you really?"

"Fair enough. Now that we're on the move," Bocnic smirked at the thought of reintroducing himself, "I'm Bocnic Drewings. Most people just call me Bo for short, but refrain from joking about Hazard if you can. It's a joke that just isn't funny anymore."

"Hazard? Never heard of the place. OK, Bo, why was I in that hospital in the first place? How do you know my name, and why do you seem to think I am in danger?"

Clouds were settling into dense fog as she watched him drive the ever-changing route north. The car's headlights began reflecting off descending mist, mimicking a scene from one of the horror movies Sally had recently watched. Other cars entered the roadway, dispelling the idea completely and bringing her back to reality. It seemed like time stood still in the car as she waited for him to speak.

Bo finally broke the silence with a question of his own. "How much do you remember about what happened before you woke up today?"

"You're evading my question..."

Bo stopped her from continuing. "Just think back. It's important if I'm going to answer you."

Sally stared out the front window pondering his psychobabble answer. She thought back to what she did remember as the predawn light of morning illuminated the fog, infusing the low-lying clouds with muted shades of pink and yellow. It seemed so long ago to remember her friends visiting from California. She could not answer right away because the cobwebs cluttering her mind were thick and covered with dust. Some time passed before she got any words out. Bo sat patiently as if this sort of thing happened all the time. Once she had a firm grasp on what happened did she start her tale.

**

Friends from her college days in California had come out to visit Colorado for the first time. Sally had always made the trips out to visit them each year. Now she was twenty-six years old and assistant manager at Kmart, with the demand to get Christmas displays up earlier and earlier each year, so they would have to visit her this time. They had refused to see Colorado Springs in the past because they felt it in their collective minds that she lived in a "town" not a city. She would prove them wrong. This city had the same things they were used to in California, if they would only come to visit. She had e-mailed them a list of things they could all do. The last item was to drive up Pikes Peak before taking them to the airport. She included an important side note about the cold weather at the top and to pack warm stuff just in case.

When she went to pick them up at Denver International Airport around noon, Sally was overjoyed when they stepped off the escalators and passed the buffer zone set up by security. They spent time visiting all the sights during the day and enjoyed some of the nightlife the city had to offer. Questions popped up now and again about Sally's elusive boyfriend until she finally broke down telling them he had left for greener pastures. One of them asked her if that meant he'd died, drawing out a much-needed laugh from Sally. She cleared the air by saying he'd found someone younger, and the last words about the subject were "cradle robber."

The first cold snap of winter usually came at the end of October, but that was a few weeks away and the temperature was holding around the mid seventies normally. Their final trip took them through Manitou Springs on their way to Green Mountain Falls, where the entrance for Pikes Peak hid. It took all morning to get her friends motivated and dressed. A brief look at the Weather Channel told them the same story as yesterday: unseasonably hot weather in the upper eighties. The camera was packed along with her coat so Sally could have a record of her friends freezing even after all her pleading they dress more warmly. So it was close to lunch by the time they left, giving them an opportunity to try her favorite place. She suggested they stop in Manitou Springs for a bite at the Spice of Life Cafe and Deli; it was one of her favorite places to frequent. She could stock up on spiced butter rum coffee, making it a win-win for them all.

After the quaint atmosphere of Manitou Springs nestled in the crook of the towering mountainside, the majestic scenery up the mountain pass made everyone awestruck. A creek ran down the middle of the road acting like a divider for the two-way traffic, trees of all sorts dotted the area, and bared rock faces lay exposed from the excavation to pave the road up. The beautiful scenery of the mountains seemed to turn her friends into amateur photographers with an eye for everything. Reaching the end of the windy mountain pass brought them their first left turn off the main stretch of road, across from the post office, leading to Pikes Peak and the fourteen thousand foot summit. Asphalt turned into dirt as the road shifted to more of a country theme. A short while later brought them to the pearly gates at the end of their quest.

As they passed the gift shop near the entrance there was a sign noting the temperature at the top would be near fifty degrees. "Shouldn't be that bad up there," one of her friends stated. She only laughed; if the wind was blowing it would be colder.

A ranger stood just outside the entrance with what appeared to be a meat thermometer in one hand while he used the other to stop vehicles. Sally told them he was there to check the temperature of the brakes before letting any car precede the rest of the way down the mountain. She calmed their fears about the climb up, after explaining yet again how she had made this trip many times before without a single problem. She always left out the fact that the Pikes Peak Hill Climb race ran these same roads at high speeds because the roads could be that dangerous.

The surrounding hills were beautiful to view from the safety of the car. Breaking away from the tree line of aspens, firs, and pine trees made the rest of the way up appear to look like a desert; nothing grew at this altitude. Few cars passed them heading down the zigzag dirt road until they reached the summit. After making it to the top unscathed, they all jumped out for a quick picture by the edge of the peak facing Kansas, a partly cloudy day as the backdrop. Wind billowed frigid blankets of air over everything before the group ran to the building for something warm to drink. Spending a little time and money browsing the shelves to buy trinkets, they figured the choice of attire might best be suited for visiting the Garden of the Gods Park instead. Lucky for them the car was parked close by. Heading down the swerving road back to Green Mountain Falls, the steering on the car became erratic, and from there it all became pitch black for Sally…

**

Her memories did not serve her as well as she had hoped, and looked to Bo for the missing answers. She floundered to think of what came next. He spoke up to ease her discomfort. Bo said mildly in a soft voice, "You were in an accident off a dirt road coming down Pikes

Peak three days ago. Because of the backlog of awaiting bodies, an autopsy had been scheduled for this morning."

"You took me from a hospital that was supposed to take care of me? From the accident I don't remember. Now I don't even know if my friends in the car made it safely?" she said heatedly. Sally's thoughts were swirling out of control. That's when Bo's last sentence hit her, "Whose autopsy? Which of…wait, I killed all of my closest friends in a car crash! Turn around now!" Fear kept her from making too many complete sentences.

Bo shook his head gently; saddened by apparently being the bearer of the bad news. "You don't understand, Sally. No one survived the crash. There weren't any guardrails. The car careened off the road and rolled for some time before hitting a tree that burst the gas tank, which then caught fire.

"You were thrown from the car since you forgot to wear your seat belt and didn't get consumed; your friends weren't so lucky. An autopsy would have happened this morning had I not sneaked in to save you. The backlog of bodies due for autopsy was two days behind schedule because of hospital layoffs. Good thing, too, because if they had had the chance to cut you open this conversation might not have happened. Besides, your body needed time to…"

She interrupted him in mid sentence to scream at the top of her lungs. Rage consumed her thoughts while she let out her primal cry only to clear her head enough to process a growing fear. She was with a madman that now had her in his car, and she did not have an inkling where this Bo was taking her. How could she have put this much trust in a person she barely knew? *There must be something I can do*, she thought to console herself. The short stint she'd served in the Army did not prepare her for rolling out of a moving car; however, she was going to put her cards on the table and just go for it. Acting like she was adjusting her seat belt with one hand, she darted her other hand for the door handle, and pulled at the same time on the seat belt catch to release the latch.

Using the seat belt as a swing, she kicked out without looking at the ground; they were moving pretty fast. She tucked into a roll after releasing the car door just before hitting the ground. The sudden impact pushed the air out of her lungs unexpectedly, bouncing her back into the night air and passed the car. Too focused on breathing again, Sally was unprepared for the next collision with hard pavement as she hit the ground quickly. Arms absorbed most of the force and her right forearm gave a sickening crack making her release one of her legs.

Stifling a scream from the pain that shot up her arm, she raised her head in time to see the light post coming at her faster than her brain was thinking. An involuntary response to the immobile object made Sally's body finish uncoiling at the wrong moment. Her body collapsed around the pole at her lower back, dislocating her lower vertebra along with shattering some ribs. She lay there having a hard time breathing through the pain of cracked ribs and unable to move; the thought of Bo scooping her up and taking her to some abandoned building to do whatever he pleased began to frighten her. Sally was in no condition to even try screaming for help anymore. The only movement she had left was her head, as she looked up to find Bo's car backing up where she now rested.

CHAPTER 3

Bo stared back in amazement through the rearview mirror. Sally had jumped from a moving car to get away from him. With her short-term memory loss as a result from dying, it was a given that she might not believe him; or maybe she was not listening and thought he was going to kill her. Either way, she could have waited until they had come to a stop light or sign before risking an escape. *If she is this spontaneous hearing about her death will she react to every situation like this?* he wondered. She might need more help than the time he had allowed for. Besides, when was the last time a newbie did bodily harm to him or herself so soon? Never.

Should have considered the ramifications of using a moving vehicle to enlighten someone freshly reborn before opening his mouth, he scolded himself. *Could have been a much better outcome.*

Bo looked again through the rearview mirror to see her motionless there on the street. He put the car in reverse to back up as close to her as he could and hopefully use the car as a shield against any onlookers that might happen by. Midway to his goal, he stopped to retrieve the sheet she'd lost during her acrobatic tumble; it had blown past her towards him in the wind. He tossed it into the passenger seat, all the while grumbling to himself about how impertinent and reckless Sally was.

When he got close enough to see better, she had not moved an inch, which either meant that wrapping herself around the light post like it was a game of horseshoes had damaged her more than he thought—or being so new might have actually killed her. The latter did not sound probable, but better to close the gap between them to know for sure. No one ever died before, so he doubted she might be the first. Still, Bo realized he had never bought it up in the past with his elders, and no one ever had said it was impossible. He brushed the thought away as nonsense to focus on backing up without running her over. Once there he rushed out of the car to be by her side, making sure Sally's Wakening didn't really end so soon.

This was the second time in so many hours that he had seen her bared naked. Because of the adrenaline pushing him to get out of the hospital, he had not paid much attention to what Sally looked like. Now Bo was focused once again on her lithe frame under the glow of the streetlamp: the long, auburn hair framing half of her face and one of the medium-sized breasts fanning the rest of her almost hourglass shaped figure, and all packed into a five-and-a-half-foot frame. Bo took in all her beauty as he looked her over for signs of life and inspected her injuries. The combination of her battered as she was and him being dead for so long kept any unwanted thoughts from ever coming to surface. She was going to be very mad after he explained how she would be fixed up.

Taking a brief look around for stray headlights illuminating the heavy fog, he scooped her up with a hand behind knees and head and laid her flat on the sidewalk. He whispered what he planned to do to help and looked into her eyes for any sign of acknowledgment of what he was about to do. Only a steady stream of tears cascaded down her cheeks, her eyes refusing to focus, and eyebrows furrowing together in confusion gave him what he needed. It was answer enough for him.

She finally gets it, Bo regretfully thought to himself. *First lessons are the hardest and I wished she would have waited to learn this one.*

"Still think you're not dead?" He jabbed with his words, hot under the collar from her stupid jump. "The way you bent around that pole should make you wish it," he sighed, "but I won't hold it against you. You're not the first to take the news so badly about your death and the memory loss to go with it; however, none of them tried to off themselves either.

"Take this as your first lesson about being undead. There are a lot of broken bones and a tumble that should have killed you, but you're not dead. Can't die, to be exact.

"Bones will have to be broken if I'm going to set them properly. I see the concern on your face, but it looks like you're paralyzed somewhere from the neck down, which is good." Bo cringed as he quickly glanced back down her body. "I have to break some bones and put sockets in the right place; however, the severed nerves will keep you from feeling most of it. That's why I'm leaving your back for last." And with that said he snapped her left forearm in half over his knee.

Bo made quick work of setting bones and popping joints back into place with assistance from the inherent healing magic within her leaving only bruising behind. Tears ran the length of her face to the concrete as he cracked her back by placing his feet on her hips while holding her head; slowly relaxing his muscles, allowing her spine to line back up and fuse together again. Sally lay there weeping after he rolled her onto her back again. Small fits of verbalized anguish spilled from her lips from apparent pain still waging war within her nerves. He made a motion to help her up, but all she had strength for was to raise her arm enough to wave him off before succumbing to gravity once more. All Bo could do was watch for traffic passing by, hoping no one stopped to inspect.

Half an hour passed as he watched a few cars drive by unaware while waiting for Sally to come to terms with her new life. The small spasms made by her muscles subsided and she stared either up to the sky or over the bridge, but never in his direction. Bo could tell she'd been brooding over the experiences just recently past.

"Most of the pain will be mental as the fresher ones heal." He wanted it to come out more apologetic. However, Sally's expression told him another story. He tried again. "You heal at a remarkable rate for being so young."

"I feel like crap! You have any aspirin in that heap to stave off the pain a while?" She attempted a menacing glare but a shot of pain ran through her as she tried to prop herself up on elbows.

"Sure, be right back."

Bo returned with the bottle of pills in one hand and a bottle of water he'd found in the back seat in the other. The sheet Sally had lost was wrapped around the arm. He handed her the sheet first followed by the pills and water, she could not help but look down at her body automatically. Her expression was pure embarrassment as she snatched the sheet away from quickly to drape it across her naked flesh. Bo turned his back yet again as she covered up and spat curses as she sat up. When he turned back around, she flashed him a brief smile before removing the lid from the bottle and shaking out a couple of aspirin.

Sally relented this time when Bo reached out again to help her up from the curb with moans of pain to mark the effort. He slowly walked her to the car's front bumper for support as she leaned on him heavily.

"The magic's very strong at such an early stage," Bo commented, a bit bewildered himself about her quick recovery. "Can't say I know of anyone who healed as fast as you have—a little wobbly maybe but otherwise whole. Quite remarkable really since no one else that I know has ever risen and then tried to commit suicide." He finished with a smirk.

"I thought you were going to kill me! What else did you expect me to do?" she said hysterically.

Sally looked like she was regaining strength as she attempted to push away from the hood. Bo wanted to move closer for support, but she flashed determined eyes his way that kept him from moving. She fell back to the hood with a loud thud, breathing hard from trying too soon to move.

Bo tried to reassure her. "That weakness should pass soon. No need to rush it along when there isn't anything out here chasing us. The healing will be done soon enough, and the pain will wash away with it."

She took a few deep breaths before placing the palms of her hands on the hood and repeated the attempt again. *Stubborn, that's what she was*, Bo thought with as he smirked inwardly.

He was glad to see there was not as much effort this time with less show of pain, but that might just be for his benefit. Using her right hand to steady herself, Sally stood, precariously close to falling, but she stood nonetheless. A few more deep breaths, which showed Bo she was not without pain, gave her the courage to take a step away from the car, then another to make sure the first was not an illusion.

Looking up from her small accomplishment with a smile, however, seeing Bocnic caused it to melt away. He could tell it was him that jarred her back to reality. She set eyes on him, poised to speak but he noticed her pause with mouth slightly opened as if considering what or how she was going to phrase her next words. They came out rushed.

"Ritual? Who did that to me and why?"

Bo did not want to spook her again even though she seemed to accept what was happening a little better. He would have to keep from tripping over his own tongue a bit more by watering down the information for her. "We're not talking about some shaman standing over you chanting, if that's what you think. It's more like the Powers-That-Be out there drawing energy around your body to breathe life back into it. There are some theories explaining why we even exist in the first place, but let's just say you're here and be happy with that. Safer that way in most circles if you don't try bringing your own ideas into the mix.

"The ritual itself is quite beautiful under the cast of the moon with the soulful essence of light floating about until it rests back on the body for the rebirth. But I wouldn't stand too close if you have the chance to see it, as the light forming in the area could draw out your own essence as well, and you don't want that happening." He looked around nervously before pointing to the car. "Could we have this conversation while we drive?"

Sally tilted her head. "Sure, if you trust me not to jump again." That brought a laugh from them both as they climbed into the car.

Feeling at ease now that they were back on the road, Bo continued, "As for your own body, it will continue to think it's alive for some time and everyday things will still need to be done, like eating once a day minimum, bathroom use because of the eating, and other normal things life threw at you before converting until you grow into your new life. The cold, hunger, general pain like when you stub your toe, and the like will also haunt you until that finally passes on, too. Mostly, that sort of stuff can be shoved aside by using a simple mind trick to overcome and ignore your surrounding or pain.

"When you break something like when you broke your back, the healing begins fairly fast, and you shouldn't be incapacitated for long before moving again, which is a good thing in a bad situation. If you get knocked unconscious, it won't last long, I hope." Bo's voice faded as he considered her rapid healing and compared it to other undead he knew. She had a knack for healing, it seemed.

From the corner of his eye, he saw Sally twitch a little like she was fending off the tingling sensation you get from a feather down the spine. Aftereffects from the healing, to be sure. Once she was settled back in she asked, "Why me?"

That was always a good question, Bo thought. He had wondered the same thing since he'd turned before giving up on finding an answer. There was not anything else to tell her except, "I don't know."

He spoke rapidly, avoiding Sally's temper from boiling over and losing her before he could teach her anything else, "Each person is born with a unique gift for various uses. For myself, I see magic being used or what is left of it when a spell is done. That doesn't explain why you or the undead exist at all, but we believe all things in life need a balance and we supply that need. One theory says our role might be to police the supernatural world for spikes offsetting the fragile balance between good and evil, one species of supernatural beings dominating another, or even the world. Beyond that we all seem to become without knowing why.

"This is your rebirth to a new kind of life, as the Church would tell it, but it's the same concept in both cases. Religion says life has purpose, but no one will tell you what that purpose is. Same deal now except no religious subtext to follow.

"Moving on to something more important. Undead have rules just like any other culture might. We keep to ourselves, no telling others about your 'condition,' and every forty years give or take there is a certain drink that must be taken to keep up the appearance of the living, or you begin to take on the look of those horror movie zombies," he concluded as Sally sat restless in her seat. She appeared to be getting antsy and he felt it, too. "Let's get back to the motel without any more of that stunt driver training you pulled, and I can finish up filling you in about the rest of it, OK?"

"Clothes first. I'm not running around town in a sheet no matter how sexy it makes me look. I must have left my purse at home, so you'll have to buy them for me, and don't get any ideas about what I should be wearing either," she said with a wink, feeling a lot more relaxed with the thought jeans and a shirt between her and the world.

They drove off to find a Wal-Mart just over the bridge on Eighth Street buying her a few sets of clothes. Bo had to do all the shopping, as her appearance would draw too much again, and surveillance cameras might pick up her image for someone to identify her. With her sizes in hand, he went to the task of shopping. In no time flat he finished and brought the bag to the backseat. "I was *not* picking out bras for you. You'll have to deal with the sixties look until we can have you do that part."

Sally graciously took the bag and asked him to stand guard outside while she slipped into the new clothes. He had already seen what she looked like naked twice, but it was the principle that mattered. The car shook from the effort as she struggled in the backseat with her pants before knocking on the glass to let him back in the car.

They made it to the motel Bo had rented in advance and brought her things to the room. He sat down on one of the twin beds while she took the other. "Do you need a drink before I start again? There's a vending machine down the hall a few rooms away," he asked.

At the mention of anything tangible, her stomach answered back for her with a large rumble. "Diet anything and some fat-free chips if that's all right," she answered.

"I'll be right back." He grinned as the door closed on his own inside joke.

A few minutes later the door opened; Bo had two drinks and some bags of chips for each of them. As he handed her the stuff he bought, she exclaimed, "This isn't what I asked for."

"Something you should get used to from the get go is that 'diet' anything won't help you now. Your body is locked in the state it is from here on out. Right now you will need what extra the 'fatty' food can do for you after that healing your body was forced to perform so soon. Get used to it, and even enjoy the fact food now can have flavor." The last part brought a small smile to his face as he waited for her reaction.

Sally sat staring at the drink and chips as if contemplating what to do. "Thanks," she said sounding defeated.

Resolute that she was going to be a hard case, he tried to soothe her. "Your body had to burn essential resources to mend the broken bones and heal any torn flesh. What is used has to be replenished, or the body will become weaker. By no means will it kill you; however, you will have less to work with if there is a need to use a fight-or-flight reaction your body is born with to protect yourself." These speeches always felt like he was talking to child in class who didn't want to listen, staring out the window forlorn with the playground.

Sally opened the bag with a sigh and started eating chips one at a time like there were vipers in the bag ready to snap at her in an instant. Soon the fear that drove her to living the fat-free life vanished, and she devoured the bag. Popping open the soda, she began to guzzle, and Bo had to put a hand on the can almost forcing her hand back down with some effort. "Ease off, it's not going anywhere and neither are you. With the need your body is calling out for and the fact of you feeling this is a guilty pleasure, it will only hurt you in the end. Take it slow and the body will let you know when to stop…"

"But it is so good!" She interrupted him in mid-sentence. "I had forgotten just what it was like to not have the aspartame aftertaste to virtually everything I ate, but now I'm going to need another one of those bags if you're not going to eat it."

Bo handed her another bag and sat back down to consider the next thing he might tell her. There was just so much to lay out in a very short time. The problem of letting out too much information was what she might let slip or blatantly say in a room of eavesdroppers. With the alarm clock between the beds reading just after two in the afternoon, Bocnic felt pressed for time. It was a feeling he had not shook since the light pole fiasco, and it would not hurt to report back to camp about Sally being safe.

He watched her put a hand to her stomach in response to a rumbling inside. "I don't want to impose more than I have to, but I think chips and soda aren't going to cut it. Can we order something in, if that's OK?"

"Sure, what'll it be?"

"Pizza with everything," she told him almost too fast to believe she had even spoken.

"I kind of thought you might say that. Hold on while I make the call, and then we'll get back to the handbook of the dead."

CHAPTER 4

"What of the target?"

His voice resonated within the confines of the wide expanse of the room. Pillars reached up from the floor supporting twenty foot ceilings. Speckling the room's floor around each pillar base leaned rare treasures collect over the centuries. The man being questioned was casually leaning against one of the many pillars in the room, and chewed his lower lip as if considering the question unwarranted. The man questioning him knew just as much as he did to date, yet asked stupid questions anyway. If he did not have to report to this impertinent bastard and the rest of the church heads so often, there might be headway made on finding his target and the rest of its kind.

Demric Longshoff, head priest to The Cross, was charged with running an extended branch of the church that replaced the Inquisition's misaligned purpose. Its true intent of killing abominations on God's green earth had always been hidden beneath its search to convert people.

Near the point of spitting the words, Demric spoke out: "Little more has become evident since the target's demise. Our top men have been dispatched to Colorado overseeing the search personally. They'll send a report later today from the two major cities." It felt like such a waste of his time relating all this to the man, but he went on anyway. "This state is the closest we could narrow down to finding the target's location. They've started in Denver and Pueblo moving from there to smaller cities until there is no other place to hide."

His superior waved him on showing the boredom Demric felt. "Nothing more was gained from the Temerdon's pointing pendulum. It can only show the vicinity where undead have risen and the updates we've made to the maps since the inquisition haven't proven all that accurate."

"Is there anything else?"

"Besides floundering at every step? There's only so much we have to work with. Have we not proven ourselves in the past to be resourceful?" Demric finally spat out in such a contemptuous voice. The other man ended up showing signs of agitation at being talked down to.

"Very well, contact me again when we have a name," his superior said in an off-handed tone, then moved away as if the conversation had never happened.

Obstinate bastard, Demric thought to himself as he moved off in the opposite direction to the passage leading lower beneath the church. The church's political face nowadays was one of redemption and salvation, when the real work to cleanse the world happened in dark alleys and midnight raids on the unholy. When would his so-called leaders acknowledge that their religion ran side by side with these abominations conducting sacrifices to appease a foreign god? He rambled on in his own head with fuming thoughts as he descended the stone spiral staircase to his true work and the catacombs. Once in his office, the door secured behind him, Demric moved to the cluttered desk fingering through the various piles of paper in search of a name to a contact.

Muffled voices struck up from the next room. "Shut up! Remember the last time your incessant screeches got on my last nerve? I am not in the mood to deal with you now," Demric bellowed, and the voices ceased. He would move them if there was a safer place, but having them close to kick around also helped him through the bad days after dealing with the church heads.

He sat down, a sigh escaping his lips as his shoulders sagged. Along with the paperwork that should have been filed were a pen cup and an antique desk lamp with a pair of golden handcuffs dangling from it. The contacts, or spies for lack of a better word, for different countries would be too easy to find if filed in one location, so he had a very complicated system strewn across his desk. He smiled deeply as his eyes lit upon the name in question, Mike from the middle of the US. He had not heard from him for some time, and the question was why, Demric pondered. Michal never liked being called Mike, but it was a little joy he gained every time they spoke. There must have been a good reason for Mike not calling with a name of the target. The mobile units were due to check in soon, but fresh air and coffee would clear his head in the meantime.

CHAPTER 5

Earlier while waiting for the pizza to arrive, Sally and Bo had alternated taking showers. They both needed it needed it badly, what with her blood on him and the grit from the road all over her. Now that the pizza was delivered they had wasted no time setting up a fake pizza bar across the dresser top with the two boxes Bo ordered. With Sally occupied by hot melted cheese trying to escape the rest of the pie, Bo took the opportunity to start the conversation back up.

"Exposure to full daylight can drain the powers of the undead substantially in the newly converted. You'll have something to work with, but not much," he carried on in a lecturing tone. He would not be around after a day or two, so she had to be crammed to the brim before then.

"So I can do magic, not just be magical?" Sally asked with eyebrows raised.

"Well, yes. Practicing magic is a learned skill, whereas your body is magical itself and will take care of you without your intervention. The magic you can weld comes from all around. If you have to picture it you might think of a giant sea, ebbing and flowing, always in moving in relation to the sun instead of the moon; like the coastal tides. Also think of your body as a battery holding a given amount of charge. That battery can and will be depleted with use and will have to be recharged similar to a trickle charge a car generates. For you the magic will start out small and grow as time passes." Clearly frustrated by her interruption, he went on, "Let's stick to what can hinder you before covering anything else, OK?"

"OK, mouth shut from here out—or I'll do what I can with stuffing the pizza in my gullet."

He relaxed a little by the way she spoke. Bo hoped flashing a smile would let Sally know there were no hard feelings. He paced the room's small walkway between the door and bathroom gathering his thoughts once more.

Apparently satisfied she would keep quiet he continued, "Graveyards are a place to stay well clear of altogether. They have the power to pull in the undead. Once an undead sets foot past the gates, they will be put in a state of endless sleep, or to the outside world they appear dead, until they're removed from the grounds." His voice had the sternness of a father speaking to a child. "Just getting close to one will make you wish for sleep, which is a good warning sign a cemetery is close."

"I promised not to interrupt again, but graveyards? Really?" Sally refrained from laughter as best she could at the thought of undead and cemeteries. Everything Bo said to this point was out-of-this-world, but graveyards knocking out undead sounded a bit extreme.

"As funny as it sounds it's true," he replied, throwing a dismissive look her direction. "The Powers-That-Be have had many names down the centuries, but the one thing to remember is that they represent both good and evil. The graveyards are just one of the gifts the evil side gave for some semblance of balance to the immortal world."

For the remainder of the day Sally did not hold to her bargain and asked questions about everything Bo said. Anything from how the magic other creatures used worked to the different species that lived among and around human kind. She could not believe that the stories about folklore were really a kind of historical text of what once roamed openly. No evidence was ever left behind to substantiate the existence of such creatures, helping in hiding the truth. As Bo told it, vampires turned to dust when killed, werewolves reverted back to human form, and dragons burned from the inside out in a vain attempt at striking back, leaving only ash in their wake, just to name a few.

It made perfect sense that stories became fables used to scare children into behaving; nowadays a parent was hard-pressed to scare a child into anything unless it was to take the cell phone or mp3 player away. Sally's head was swimming to the point of overflowing with all the information he had shoveled into her. Bo suggested a break and she gladly took it.

Without them realizing it, dusk had set in when they took a break from his endless lecturing. The room was constantly lit by various lamps and the shades were always pulled shut in case someone recognized Sally. She made her way for the bathroom to wash off pizza grease all the while resisting urges to lick it right off her fingers, again. It was so good she wanted more, but her stomach said otherwise. Thinking back to what Bo had already talked about drew a shiver down her spine. Knowing he still had more to tell her made her visibly shake. In the midst of her wandering thoughts she began to feel dizzy and grabbed the sink for support.

A strange sensation came over her as the dizziness faded, starting from the pit of her stomach and working its way outward. It sort of felt like the days back in college when she was young and experimental, leaving her energized to take on the world. Prickling spread across her skin in waves, followed by goose bumps, while she finished regaining her balance. On top of it all a need grew stronger within her each passing second, something that she could not control or deny.

CHAPTER 6

Bo sat in a chair making notes for Sally when he noticed the room get warmer. Reaching a hand over to the air-conditioner proved it was still running; that was when he felt her presence. She stood there at the bathroom door with arms crossed beneath her breasts, head slightly tilted down in a come-hither tone, eyes locked on him. When she saw him looking back, she strutted slowly towards him taking in the room as she went.

The sun! he frantically thought. He had felt the power surge of a setting sun so many times that it had become second nature to him—but to forget now? Now Bo would have to face the consequences of that failure.

As power from sundown filled the undead they took on different attributes of human life, running the gambit from lust to hatred. Bo had just lucked out with a woman with the yearnings of a succubus. Sally moved towards him meaningfully and with determination, which left few choices. The magic was potent in her from the way she held herself, putting him in more danger of being raped or worse if he did nothing.

Jumping from the chair, he rammed an arm outward and flicked his wrist, followed by a string of incoherent words that brought her to a standstill a few feet away. Sally stood frozen in place mid-stride, the prior intent rushing out of her in visible waves of heat. Keeping his distance as best he could behind the second twin bed, Bo circled around her. Energy crackled along Sally's skin with streaks of translucent green running the length of her body. Satisfied his magic would hold, Bo made his way to the door and to the car.

Returning from the trunk, he stood at the entrance to the room, backlit by parking lot lights squashing the darkness of night, a duffle bag held in both hands. Bo dropped the bag on the closest bed to the door and unzipped it, pulling on a pair of gloves he removed gold-colored handcuffs from it. Reaching back he closed the door and secured the locks. He heard behind him in the silent room Sally trying to speak, but it wasn't possible with the spell he put on her. She shouldn't be able to do anything until he released her.

Handcuffs were the only thing in his arsenal guaranteed to snuff out the magic building in her. Movement from Sally's arms drove him to act fast with the restraints. She fell to her knees when the golden handcuffs touched her skin. Bo bent down on one knee as fast as he could to catch her shoulders, preventing Sally from performing a face plant on the floor.

Confusion riddled her face for a fraction of a second until she noticed where they headed. Bo guided her by the elbow after getting her to stand up again, leading her to the empty bed to rest. Sally was breathing hard as he laid her quivering form down, not noticing her hands near the top of his shirt until it was too late. She pulled him in for a deep kiss with longing written across her lips. He tried to defy her, but Sally had a hold of his neck powered by the influx of magic still in her, pinning him to her. At first he resisted by pressing his lips firmly shut to avoid her searching tongue. But with the strength he had Bo didn't want to hurt her by forcing himself away. She made it futile to continue refusing so he fell into the kiss.

Sally let up on her hold of him as they kissed passionately until she released his neck to stroke both sides of his face—and that was when he found the chance to pull back as fast as he could. She stopped the moment he had pulled away trying to see what he was up to, and noticed the rope Bo had brought into the room with the cuffs. A squeak of glee bound out of her as he began hooking it to one edge of the bed at the top and wrapping her in a zigzag pattern to the bottom. After finishing his work he sat down on the opposite bed and glared at her.

"What is it with women and sex? I know men want it all the time, but women..." He trailed off as Sally attempted to break free. "If I were alive there would be no stopping me after the way you acted. That was a long time ago, and being dead kills the urge. Don't take it the wrong way, I'm not giving in, but I never got the chance to tell you about sunsets and what might happen. I'm stepping out for a moment to give you time to cool off; after I see you're better from the window I'll come back in."

"*Now* you want to tell me? Are you sure you forgot, or did you just want to see me in the throes of a good sex meltdown?" She waited for a response but continued when there was none, "I thought that was why you brought cuffs and rope, but you decided to sit on the other bed…"

Bo opened the door and slammed it behind him. How stupid he had been to miss the sun going down. At least he could take the time to work out anything else she might need to know before something like this happened again.

CHAPTER 7

Sally stared at the door with a venomous glare hoping heat would eat through the door and hit Bo where it counted. The audacity of the man to put her in that kind of mood on purpose! He stayed out there for some time, allowing her to do deep breathing exercises to control the anger. She had started to feel better after he'd left the room, and she hoped it could stay that way.

No such luck; he reentered the room saying, "Should have seen this coming before it took hold of you. I'm sorry. The effects you're feeling can be different for each person, and you got slapped with lust. It looks like I'll be around for at least two more days until I'm sure you've got the hang of the 'sundown crazies,' as we fondly call it."

He had apologized. She did not have the mental fortitude to stay mad any longer. "Why am I not feeling so crazy now?"

Bo looked down to her wrists. "The cuffs. Gold has a kind of power over the undead that draws out magic and makes us weak. Didn't you ever notice how churches are decorated with it? We know they gathered it to use against us in an effort to control the undead. They did that to hide their true purpose behind the gold and to keep some on hand if any uprisings occurred from our kind. In the past Churches used gold to enslave us for building chapels and cathedrals. Good labor, like the undead, is hard to come by and people that could work forever are the best kind. By the way, how are you feeling now?"

"It was like a freight train out of control in the beginning, but now I'm back to normal. I really had no control over anything I did or thought, and I wouldn't want that feeling back," she said, ferreting out some dignity.

"Nothing to be embarrassed about when you haven't been trained," Bo attempted to say in soothing tones. "That's why I'm sticking around a little longer, that and to understand why the gold had no lasting effect on you. Gold is as strong a deterrent as any to mute undead magic, and you kept going like the energizer bunny." He scratched his head musing over that one.

Clearly feeling the urge to enlighten her again, he began, "Gold back in the day was worthless, as it couldn't be used to make anything substantial like a sword or a wheel rim because it wouldn't hold up under stress. For a while it was used just for coins because it was so flimsy compared to the other metals. Then, I don't know how, the Egyptians found it had qualities against certain types of supernatural beings and took gold up in droves. After that, we had a revolt to free the enslaved and to rid them of any gold they had left. The undead that ran from the pharaohs became great myths in their own right, and to this day movies are made about mummies, and later it became zombies.

"The religions that followed kept the tradition alive by incorporating gold into their idols and icons, such as the cross, as a form of showing wealth; however, there still were some that knew what the gold was used for and continued to hunt us down. Two examples are the Inquisition and the Salem Witch Trials—separate religions under the same God. Both were to ferret out the undead and supernatural in order to cleanse the earth of ungodly creatures."

Sally made movement to interrupt, but he stopped her in her tracks. "Not now. This might save your life. We aren't certain which one out of the multiple branches aligned under a single God has it out for us these days. The men working for the Church don't wear a sign proclaiming their dedication, although it was the Catholic Church that did most of the hunting in the past. The Church still hunts the undead today, and these cuffs you wear are from their stock.

"Some of these churches also put graveyards next to places of worship to keep away the undead. So stay clear of churches in general. Any questions will have to wait while I take a breather out in the cold, and then I will untie you, but the cuffs stay on for a couple more hours," Bo finished with a sigh. "The rush of power that will come back after I remove the cuffs might put you back where you started. We'll practice funneling the magic into your body for now. Do you feel drained of power right now?"

"No, just feel like I did before this whole mess started up."

She moved around on the edge of the bed to demonstrate she felt. Bo wasn't so sure he believed her and felt uneasy at the answer.

**

Days later after rehashing what he had already told her and only after he seemed to feel she could handle herself better during sunsets did Bo give Sally her traveling money to relocate. Friends and family were not to be contacted.

Bo tilted his head at her saying, "I hate to say it, but I have to move on. You're versed enough now in how to conduct yourself with the general public and to keep a low profile."

Bo added sheepishly. "Cabin fever feels like its setting in and I can't sit around in one place for too long. Never have been able to. We'll meet up again sometime in the future I am sure."

She was sad to see him go; he had rescued her and taught her the fundamentals of being undead. There was a bond growing between them that felt like family to her now and she thought it might be the other reason Bo wanted to leave—he did not like being tied to anything or anyone it seemed. Anyway, he said he had a friend in Grand Junction to meet up with for his report and to catch up on any news of undead involvements. Bo said happy trails to her, took his few belongings, and jumped into his car. A few tears dotted her cheeks from saying goodbye after she pushed the door closed.

The longing for Bo's continued presence brought up memories of her own family she could never contact again. Friends she could never again confide in. Waves of emotion cascaded over her bringing Sally to her knees. Loss, abandonment, and betrayal were only a few of the thousands of feeling rushing in at her from all sides. Collapsing against the bed, she drew up her knees, hands brought up to cover the onslaught of fresh tears. Bouts of sobbing slowly died off as she regained control of her emotions. *I'll never be completely over missing my friends and family, but I thought I would have handled this better*, she consoled herself with. *At least I have pictures of those fond memories with my friends and family stashed online to look back on.*

Those sobering thoughts made Sally wonder where to go now that she was alone. With her head back into the game, she knew she had more money in that backpack he left than she had ever seen in one place before at her disposal. Sally had some locations for finding other undead encampments along her travels if the need arose thanks to Bo, yet what use was it all if she could not move where a friendly face was? Bo had told her for the first couple of years she would still feel like a living person with concern for weather changes, pain, and emotional spikes—which was why he'd left the handcuffs behind.

With nothing better to do, Sally sat down at the desk and pulled out the pad of paper Bo had used to make some sort of plan for her personal eternity. First thing to do was shop. She was glad Bo had picked the city of Security to get a motel. Since she rarely ventured out this far, there was a slim chance of crossing paths with any friends while she made her rounds picking up clothes for the coming winter, at least she hoped so. Sally had thought Bo did not want her to leave the room because he was so focused on getting her mind fitted for her new life as one of the undead, but when she finally turned on the TV for the first time since the hospital, she saw the reason. *He must have known the whole time to keep me locked up in the motel room.* Sally now maddened by the thought, *Absentminded men!*

The afternoon news broadcast was just starting and after sifting through some of the other channels went back to the first one. Sally sat through some of the national news until the local stuff came on, and she was priority one on their list. She was listed as a missing person. The report continued to explain how Sally Mertill was in a car accident on Pikes Peak and presumed dead; however, she could not be found at the hospital and authorities assumed she got up and walked away, which they claimed was a rare occurrence but did happen. A nurse commented on a female leaving through the front doors wrapped in a white dress. She realized later it was a bedsheet because the lady did not have shoes on and must have been in a state of confusion. She did not respond to the nurse's pleading and return to the hospital.

Sally was now in a panic about stepping foot outside the motel door ever again. How was she going to move about town without someone pointing and remarking about her resemblance to a woman on TV or calling in for a reward? Too bad Bo had left so soon; he could have gone for hair dye and makeup to help her out, and she could not figure out why this had not come up sooner. It just was not on the list of priorities at the time when monsters and killer churches seemed to take up their time. If they had watched the news reports before now this might have come up. Now she was on her own in this.

Going to the bathroom she found an unused disposable razor, toothpaste, and other complimentary items left by the motel staff. Looking into the mirror was a bad choice since she found a ghost of her former self looking back. Her hair was disheveled, rings were starting to form under her still young eyes, and it all gave her an overbearing feeling of depression. Still, she started to form a plan of action that went against her inner vanity.

She turned on the radio to distract herself from her task; the song in the background was "Duality," Slipknot singing about being insane, a state she seemed to think she was in right now. Sally reluctantly entered the bathroom again and broke open a plastic razor to expose the blades, which would have to be her scissors. The haircut ended up more of a bob style cut. She had no other choice available than the toothpaste to create more of a dreadlock look in lieu of hair dye.

After about an hour, and one more quick glance into the mirror to check the Frankenstein she had created, Sally was satisfied she could walk among the public again unnoticed, maybe.

CHAPTER 8

Sally had learned to feel when the sun rose or set and to control the "crazies" that came with it. Opening the door in broad daylight was like a freight train on the express track in her eyes. Glasses were the first thing she wanted to buy. Without a car, she would have to do her shopping in stints to gather up what she could and trek back to the motel repeatedly. The thought crossed her mind of using a shopping cart to roam store to store, but what would she do with all the stuff she had brought along the way?

Sally walked into the first place she came to, a Walgreen's, gathering up the most basic of needs and those blessed sunglasses. She threw in hair dye for a better change to her hair, toothpaste to replace what she used because Bo said even undead get bad breath, deodorant for her slowly dying body, makeup, and other items she could pack away easily. As she spotted a clothing store across the street Sally couldn't pass up a chance for another change of clothes—*a woman always has a need for options*, she repeated in her head. That's when Sally noticed someone on a bicycle roll by. It dawned on her a person didn't need a driver's license for one of those. She remembered sadly that she no longer had an identity in society without a driver's license to prove it. Not letting it get in the way of her revelation, Sally let the simple thoughts of riding a bike take over.

Strolling forward with an added spring to her step, she took the time now to look around, noticing the day was a pristinely clear, beautiful one, bringing back memories of relaxing in Memorial Park with her now very ex-boyfriend. A nice lunch spread out on a blanket for the two of them. He had left her some months ago, and Sally was in between relationships, but the thought drew a pang to her heart knowing days like those might never come again.

Every store she walked into brought a small terror of being noticed that she forced herself to get over fairly quickly, even with the knowledge of surveillance cameras taking her image. This might end up being a problem she'd figured out too late. After leaving the Walgreen's is when the round mirrors gave her pause about entering another store, but she had little choice if she was to get what she needed for the eventual departure of Colorado Springs.

Don't look up, Sally told herself timidly as she entered a clothing store. She found her selection of clothes and started to browse the racks. Sally might have had a lot of money to live off of; however, it would only go so far, so clearance aisles and charity drop-off stores were the ticket. She grabbed a handful of clothes her size and moved to the dressing rooms hoping everything would fit the first time round.

In the dressing room, Sally felt a little more normal. A deep intake of breath followed by a longer sigh relaxed her down to her toes. Now she was ready to begin trying on the various selections. Near the end of being some quick-change artist action, she caused a whirlwind clothes to fly off hangers hoping to be back in the motel room soon.

While removing the last pair of pants she noticed spotting, a sure sign of her period beginning. *I'm dead! You have got to be kidding me*, she exclaimed in her head. *To bleed even after...*

Then she remembered what Bo had said. The living part of her body would continue on as if nothing had ever happened until the magic's grip fully took effect. Sally had not given a second thought to what he had meant until now. Good thing there was a store on the way back to the motel room to stock up before making a return trip out.

Damn, I sure hoped this magic takes up residence before the next cycle started, or I'm going to be pissed. Bad enough to have this happen each month while I was alive, but undead, too? What else did she have to look forward to that she'd neglected to remember? Would her hair still need to be shaved, and would it come back? Well, if it did it was a good thing now that she had butchered the haircut; that would grow back some at least.

Paying no mind to the last pair of pants she tried on, she got dressed in her old clothes and took what she had to the counter to see if they would hold them. A quick run to the bathroom after leaving the counter revealed not a single sanitary anything for her situation. In frustration, Sally paid the cashier and headed back to the Walgreen's, all the while mumbling angrily under her breath, directing it mainly at Bo for his lack of ovarian disclosure. Finally making it back to the room, she jumped straight into the shower again to remove the rock-hard toothpaste that had baked in the sun. Her temper subsided under the refreshing water concerning Bo. She only had herself to blame. He tried to warn her without embarrassing the crap out of her.

Refreshed by a hot shower and a new coat of paint for her hair, Sally felt like a new woman. A new world awaited her with open arms, as long as that same world did not know she was undead. Living a life where no one could know her bothered Sally in a way she could not put a finger on; it drew out tears for a short time before she gained control of her emotions. *Must be my period kicking the emotions on high.*

Maybe tomorrow would be better, and she might take the time to shop for a bike. Personal items back at her apartment gave Sally a plan. The idea of going back to her apartment to seek out the landlord as Sally's twin sister crossed her mind. Would it work? She might have to wait a little longer before attempting that if the police were still looking for her missing body. What was she going to do with all of her things when she would be on the move...store it, maybe? Her family was sure to take care of it all. Most likely store it for her while her name sat on a missing person's roster.

Dinner swam through her thoughts. She hadn't stopped all day for a real meal. At the thought of food her stomach sounded off right on cue. Sally didn't want fast food for the simple reason of watching her diet—or could she really trust Bo's words and not care? If the magic did its job regulating her weight gain or loss to become virtually nonexistent issue, then she could eat whatever she chose. Going to a restaurant with some healthy choices wouldn't hurt in the meantime. No need to risk growing out of the clothes she'd just bought without knowing how her body might react to a massive calorie intake.

After dinner, with a satisfying feeling she had not had in some time, Sally headed back to the motel without one person gawking or pointing at her about seeing her face on the TV. She still felt limiting her movement outside until she was ready might be the best course of action for now. Happily fulfilled with her activities for the day, she was now worn out and tired. She had not felt this way while Bo was around and chalked it up to adrenaline overload. Guess she could find the time to lie down for the night and recoup until sleep was no longer an issue. On her way back she stopped to buy a laptop and a few other gadgets to assist in planning where her next move would be. She was glad the motel offered free internet service to help with searching out a new home. Sally wasn't happy at the thought of living like an outlaw for the rest of her...well, forever.

CHAPTER 9

Surrounded by spruce and pine trees, Mathyas stood staring up at the star-filled night laid out as if diamonds were spread across a jeweler's black velvet display cloth. As the chief to the southern clan in the Rocky Mountains region, it was his duty to locate and educate any newly undead within his borders. He stared out, bothered tonight by reports of Church movement in the Denver area, including sightings of Molthah, ferret-like animals used to hunt down the undead, being unloaded at the Denver International Airport.

How they knew there was an awaking ritual preformed was beyond him; the fact they mobilized so quickly disturbed him more. What did they know that he didn't? There was no fear of The Cross, as they liked to be known, entering those forested lands, as wards kept out even the most curious. The lands themselves were acquired back when Mathyas ordered some of his members to claim falsified documents and pose as officials up for election. The goal was to enter the everyday lives of the living with the sole purpose of infiltrating their political system. With undead in official positions, they started setting land aside creating a safe haven for the supernatural world. Now the Church was hard-pressed to enter any secluded area for fear they might become the prey.

Thoughts drifted back to the girl. *Yes*, he thought, *I could almost taste the girl's essence in the air that named the newly risen, a female.* The signs that foretold her coming weren't like any other he had witnessed, but each sign had always been unique to the person and he didn't bother paying any closer attention. Now he wondered if that was a mistake. He would have to speak with Zemra, their local witch, when she returned from doing whatever a witch does alone in the woods.

Mathyas had always had a short temper for as long as he could remember, but this action the Church took burned his wick at both ends. He would have to call a meeting for all the highest ranking members of his clan to convene in the great hall, a place dug deep below the earth. Digging out living quarters provided minimal buildings above ground to hide the camp's location, because of random flyovers by the forestry department in their search for wild fires. Once gathered they would have to decide what to do about The Cross. Word would spread fast, and time seemed against them.

Only the most skilled in masking the undead scent from Molthah could be sent out to watch movements The Cross made. Like any good chess game, it became a waiting game to see what the next move would be.

CHAPTER 10

She dreamed. At first it seemed to be images blurred and out of touch, other times flashes of memories crossed her mind's eye. Feelings of horror, screaming, and disillusioned tragedy swirled in an abyss among the beautiful, transient warmth. Some semblance of focus formed as Sally found herself in a deeply shadowed forest. It was not quite dusk, yet dawn didn't seem to be coming anytime soon, nor were there signs that the ambient light filtered by a blanket of dense fog could even emanate from the sun. Feeling eyes on her was ever-present, lurking just beyond reach of her sight through murky trails of mist. She couldn't see anything moving between the trees, but she could feel more gathering within the shadows.

A din of voices also sought her out in the distance, raised conversation with higher-pitched yelling beyond the brush and thicket of trees. She envisioned a possible shouting match by a family on vacation, trying to ward off any ideas there was something more menacing behind the sounds; before she could take a step towards the noise, she was there. The ghostly presence followed her, but she could not find where it hid. Sally stood in a clearing somewhere deeper in the forest. Mountainous peaks jutted up on either side cradling the clearing in its embrace. The edge of the tree line bubbled black with malignant shadows appearing to flow like spilled ink between the trees. She almost imagined the ink blot to look as if it was a breathing thing, bringing a chill down her spine.

What's going on, Sally thought, terrified by the new scene unfolding before her. The faces of the people were awash in clouds of vibrant colors, each a different color of the rainbow, effectively masking their features and leaving her lost to who they might be. It was obvious there was a woman held captive at the center by men holding either arm while another man stood by a podium, pronouncing some sort of sentence upon her as she screamed. The judge pointed at the woman, screaming, "Guilty!" and the men holding her pulled. A crowd Sally hadn't noticed before swarmed closer. A frenzied chant for the lady's death. The two men pulling at her arms did not seem to be doing the job this mob wanted, and a rush of people moved in.

Hands scraped at her body, fingernails dug deep into the flesh, and her screams could be heard echoing through the hollowed crevice of the canyon. Sally yelled at the top of her lungs for them to stop this madness, but no one listened. She tried to close her eyes against the horror, but the woman's cries for help forced her to open them back up.

When her eyelids lifted she found herself staring up at all the faceless people, hands groping, teeth digging deep to the bone. She was the one now screaming from the pain; it had always been her screaming. She was the one who had been on trial. She was found guilty for some crime they claimed she committed. Blood dripped from many of the mouths around her. Her left arm finally pulled free making a sucking sound from air entering the ball joint breaking free.

The scene flickered like a bad transmission on a TV show then blurred until she found herself floating in a glass ball of luminescent, colored gases. Phantom pain riddled her body even after the relief of seeing she no longer was broken and bloody settled in. Lightning struck out from all directions with no apparent starting point. Just when she was going to call out for help, a hand thrust through the mist-like gas. She stretched out to grab the hand as an anchor, no matter who it might be, when a stray bolt struck her outreached hand and sent her barreling towards the glass. The turbulent new world she found herself in shattered at the lightest touch from her body, making the glass burst apart.

Sally abruptly woke with panic bating her breath. She still felt the fear underlying the dream, but it left her with a feeling of impending doom. Death and dismay hung deep in the air as she fought to return her breathing back to a familiar rhythm. It felt like a warning of sorts, the meaning of which she could not fathom. Sleeping now was not an option. She looked at the clock radio on the nightstand seeing it was only five in the morning. *No reason to close my eyes now*, she thought solemnly, *might as well get up and ready for the day*.

Sally turned the radio on to have something to do while showering, but the song playing at that moment—"Warning" by Incubus—dragged her back to the little radio, remembering her nightmare. She wasn't one to believe in karma or any other religious mojo, but it still made her stop and wonder if this was some sort of coincidence of fate or a premonition. Switching off the bedside radio after being spooked from the choice of song they played, she opted to pick up her little waterproof mp3 player, loaded with music from the laptop she'd bought, taking it in the shower instead. Better to focus on the day's events than a bad dream.

CHAPTER 11

Bo swung the door wide, searching the interior for any signs of life. The motel room was small enough to see with one sweep of his eyes: nothing. He bounded into the room checking space between the two beds but finding only discarded clothes. Sally wasn't there, but in his haste Bo neglected to hear the sound of running water coming from the bathroom. He stopped to take the proverbial breath and calm down, whether he breathed or not. The few days he'd been gone showed in the shopping spree Sally apparently went on. Her room was littered with an explosion of bags and purchases all over the floor and spare bed. *It's going to take a lot of time to pack up*, he thought pessimistically.

Recent events made him return to help get her out of town and hidden until the crisis was over. Half the morning was already gone. The best thing to do was at least start dumping all of her things in the car trunk while she finished up.

He went in and out of the motel room carrying Sally's purchases when on a return trip for another armful the bathroom door opened. She walked through the doorway wearing ear buds with a cord connecting what he figured was an mp3 player around her neck, and nothing else. Quietly singing the song to herself, she looked up and screamed, flailing around vainly to cover herself up. Red-faced and embarrassed she stormed back to the bathroom, for a towel, he guessed, slamming the door behind her. He busied himself with picking up the rest of her things, minus a few set of clothes for her to choose from. As he walked out the front door again, Bo hollered over his shoulder for her to alert him when it was safe for this pervert to come back in.

Sally took longer than was really necessary to get dressed, probably to make him wait outside for as much time as she could manage, before letting him back inside. He leaned against the car's hood until she opened the door allowing him back in.

"The Church is coming," Bo started off after he closed the door behind him, "and they are on the hunt. To be more specific, The Cross is after you in particular. As I told you before, they are a sect of the Church that has been hunting the supernatural for some time now."

She looked flabbergasted at hearing The Cross was in her state. Sally appeared to be for a loss for words at the prospect of being hunted down like an animal. Bo wasn't sure what made Sally so special to draw their attention so fast and maliciously? The Cross came into play when a threat the Church feared arose and needed eliminating. He watched her struggle with questions floating in her head being unanswered by the expressions she made.

One of those questions finally made it passed her lips though: "If they're out to get me and if I can't die then is the hunting just like a trophy kill?"

"Worse, they divide you up into pieces so you can't heal, and I've heard they hold back a part of the body to keep the undead from being whole. The most obvious would be to take the head, keeping the body from fully being functional. However, you haven't been around a decapitated head to know that it can be more hassle than it's worth. With nothing else to do, the head of an undead will just talk for days nonstop." Sally was staring at him in disgust. "Don't start making judgment calls like that…yet. I know I didn't cover this with you earlier because I knew how you would react."

"What else did your almighty, self-righteous thinking leave out?" Sally spouted with each word heated to the point of boiling.

"Plenty, but now isn't the time to go over it. They're in Colorado and we need to be on the move," and with that he started picking up what was left to put in the trunk. "Might not be a bad idea to stuff you in there, too, instead of being berated the whole drive," he muttered on the way out the door. Sally stomped a foot and a loud huff for an answer to his comment.

Pulling away from the motel, Bo noticed Sally looking back at the room she'd stayed in as if it were the last home she would have. He had no idea when she might feel that way about anything again, but he knew those feelings could faded with time. Right now, he had to concentrate on the here and now.

Bo considered his options: if the Church was finishing up in their Denver search, then the smart thing to do would be to head that way. Or, they could go south and keep going. The Cross should have had enough time to rifle through people that had recently died around the same time Sally had. They should be on the move to the next city for inspecting those morgues by the time they reached Denver's city limits. It sounded like the best plan to him. If the past ever proved anything, they had never been able to locate undead on the first try—but there was always a first time for anything. The way they tried to pinpoint a ritual got them pretty damn close. The undead relied on Bo to find other undead being reborn. This was the reason he got assigned to find Sally, because he had the sight. The sight let him "see" any buildup of magic required to perform during Wakenings. It became a beacon that guided him to each new undead; not so for the Church at least

Sally interrupted his thoughts. "Since you say The Cross is on my tail, I have a question that's been bothering me since you left. How was it you knew my name after I woke?" she asked, perplexed.

"Simple, each person in cold storage had a clipboard with the person's info on it. On top of that, your door dripped with the passing ritual and made it easy to find. Its part of my gift to spot the changing rituals leaves behind. I'm the obvious choice when it comes to finding and helping the newly initiated. The rest you already know." He grinned at such an odd question to bring it up now.

He stared ahead looking for the onramp to I-25 north, wondering if he should call ahead and arrange some place to stay while he found out more of the Church's movement. A quick stop at a convenience store shouldn't take too long for a call and a late breakfast for Sally. He let her know if she needed to get some breakfast now would be the best time while he stopped to make the call.

She looked up at the ceiling of the car's interior letting out an irritated laugh, "In those bags you so unceremoniously shoved into your trunk is the pay-as-you-go phone I bought." She glared at him before carrying on, "They don't need ID to get one and you didn't leave me a way to get a new identity either."

At the 7-11 convenience store's payphone, Bo finished up the call as he watched Sally exited with an armload of food and drink. When he tried to ask why so much stuff, she just tsked his comment away sounding like a spitting viper with a shake of the head for emphasis. He let it slide; no need to cause a fight before the hour-and-a-half drive to Denver. At least he'd gotten good news over the phone, bringing his spirits up a little. He hadn't used her prepaid cell phone just in case someone got a hold of the number and somehow tracked them. It was one of the reasons he never carried one. Bo headed back to the car with a plan starting to form.

As he took his seat in the car Sally proceeded to explain her plentiful bounty. "I know the trip is short, but these are incidentals if something goes wrong and we can't stop."

She had a point there. If the Church found some reason to turn around for a second look, they could indeed be circling the city to keep out of reach. As they pulled out of the parking lot, the sunlight bounced off an oncoming car's windshield gave a brief moment of blindness to Bo. The cloudless sky would make the sun unrelenting from the passenger window on the drive up.

Passing through Old Colorado City on their way to I-25, they headed on the journey north to the capitol. Little talk passed between them until they hit Castle Rock; that was when Bo laid the plan out to stay in the morgue until darkness could hide some of their movements on their way to a secluded camp run by undead. Sally didn't look happy about returning to a morgue to do anything, but the look on her face said she understood they had very little choice.

CHAPTER 12

Denver traffic could be horrendous most of the time unless it was close to midnight, and even that wasn't always a guarantee during sporting events. *At least traffic was running smoothly today.* Sally's mild attempt at mundane thoughts evaded her. It didn't banish the recurring thought about being back in a morgue soon either.

They were getting close to Saint Joseph Hospital where Bo's contact worked. Bo drove around to the visitor's parking lot and found a spot near the back of the lot. A brisk wind brushed against Sally as she got out of the car when she tried to stretch her legs out. She looked over at Bo, wordlessly asking to hurry up with locking the doors to get out of the cold. He got the message.

Deep inside her a voice told Sally to run when they stepped through the sliding doors of the hospital. *It's only a building*, she repeated to herself over and over like a mantra. It did little to keep at bay the creepy feeling she had reentering a hospital so soon, but it was the most logical thing to do to hide where someone already looked.

Besides, the hospital offered food and a bed without exposing their location.

The elevator did not take long to reach. On the way down Bo briefed her, "The guy we're meeting you'll like; his name's Dirk Windlem. He doesn't like to hang around the undead much, but he agrees to help us out since we return the favor from time to time."

"What kind of favor could he need that the undead would be willing to do?" Sally asked, shock showing on her face from humans interacted with the supernatural.

"Just because you had no clue about what really lurks out there doesn't mean everyone else is just as clueless. Matter of fact, Dirk had a hit of sorts put on him by an obscure group of harpies; not many of them around, and disgusting creatures really. The upper half is human, while the lower portion looks more like a bird with hands attached at the ends of the wings mimicking a bat." Bo shook his head at the memory. "Those creatures lurk behind the alley's shadows calling out in distress when some lonely soul walks by. Tempting a person away from prying eyes.

"Dirk got assigned to do the autopsies of the victims, finding gashes across their chest and legs not typical of a mugging or murder. He started getting too close, going back to some of the crime scenes, when one of the harpies caught him peeking around too many of their hunting sites." He paused as the elevators doors opened to the hall, looking for anyone nearby before finishing the story.

"I happened across the same road Dirk was on to see him vanish down a nearby alley. I was one of a few undead patrolling the city for these pests because they were drawing too much attention with the locals for their own good. Pulling up a short distance away from the alley with my headlights off, I made it on foot just in time to see a harpy spread its wings for the killing blow."

"They just run around killing people? I remember hearing about a serial killer some time back, but I lost track to know if the guy got caught or not." Sally stared at the tiles on the floor thinking back on the report she saw. "I suppose these harpies eat bird seed?"

"Funny, no they don't." He shot her a halfhearted smirk. "Most of the time they stick to themselves hunting in the mountains. The harpies are all female; they come into heat every thirty or forty years and they need a man's seed to make fertile eggs. Anyway, it took some time to take the bird down, but that's when Dirk agreed to help us out. We saved his life, and he agreed to help us out with what he could. Dirk feels indebted to us now," Bo finished up as they entered the mortician's office.

Dirk turned from his work on the desk to stand, greeting his old friend. "Rooms are ready when you are," he said with a smile cracking his otherwise ordinary face.

Dark, short cut hair framing Dirk's clean-shaven oval face fought the gray strands taking dominance. He stood a few inches taller than Sally and was somewhat lanky in stature under the hospital greens. His appearance set Dirk near fifty in Sally's eyes.

"Dirk, I'd like you to meet Sally Mertill. Newest member of our kind with a bit of a problem, as I mentioned on the phone."

"Yes, they're still moving out of town the last I heard. Should be safe to move on to your next stop if you want," Dirk said sounding on edge. "Not that you're not welcome to stay for the time being. It'll be well after dusk when my shift ends, so I can help you two out when it's time to go."

"Sounds good" was all Bo would say. He seemed to catch a meaning Sally did not hear. She hoped their rooms really had beds.

Dirk showed them the way to the morgue's autopsy room where the storage drawers stood. Seeing the bank of drawers made Sally's skin crawl. The thought occurred to her that she might have to be crammed in with another body to keep from someone finding them, giving her reason to gag.

Dirk thought her sick noises were because of the atmosphere. "Sorry, forgot to warn you about the smell. We tend to get used to it."

"It's OK," she got out, embarrassed. She didn't smell a thing except the disinfecting cleaners used recently. Now she wondered if there really was a smell she should be getting sick from. Sally couldn't fathom her sense of smell being the first to go. Where he stopped in front shattered her hopes for any degree of comfort.

Dirk opened one of the drawers pulling out the sliding gurney. On top of the sheet laid two walkie-talkies. "I thought these might help pass some of the time while you waited." Sally gave him a questioning look. "I could've just shoved you both into one drawer and saved the money."

She got it now, no thanks to his snide remark. She could either lie in solitude or have Bo to talk with while passing the time. Her ultimate choice would have been sitting around chatting the whole time, but she didn't want to endanger Dirk's job because of her fears of being locked away in a drawer again.

"Sorry for the rush, but I have no idea when someone might return, so if you two could kindly take your places I can get back to work," Dirk said pointing to a different drawer.

He made quick work of getting them on the sliding tables and sealed in before anyone showed up. Sally wished he had thought of a flashlight, too, now that the door was closed effectively killing off any light. The space was worse than dark, pitch black didn't even cover it. Sally had fears of being claustrophobic when she had done in an MRI scan some years back. It happened when the walls interior pressed in on her as she slid into the machine. Even with the complete darkness, sounds of her shifting within the cramped space echoed off the walls, making her brain register just how little room she had. Her hand fumbled for the walkie-talkie's *on* switch, and the glow from the red indicator reflecting off the stainless steel tomb gave her comfort.

She keyed the microphone up using the toggle switch on the side. "You there?" Sally asked the silence.

No response came back from the other end. Bo must not have turned his on yet. *They should have got them working before getting locked in.* Sally's thoughts were racing, letting her know she was beginning to panic. Restraint from beating the walls for attention was hard won, however nerve-wracking the ordeal became. Not knowing who might be on the other side by now kept her from making that mistake. Sally lost track of time, feeling hours had passed in her building fright to escape. When she was about to give in to the compulsion to yell for help, a voice came from the walkie-talkie.

"Can you hear me?" Bo questioned on the other end.

"God, yes, I can. Too small in here for me. I don't know how long I can take this," she yammered back, terror rising in her voice. Sally wondered why he wasn't saying anything back, making her whimper incoherently and shake violently. Then she realized her grip was so tight on the walkie-talkie that she never released the talk button. Feeling a little stupid, she let go of it.

Sally could tell in Bo's voice he wanted to comfort her fears, "Shhh, close your eyes and take deep breaths. Think back on some happy thoughts while you inhale through your mouth and exhale out your nose. It will slow down your heart enough to calm your nerves. Best thing to do is sleep while we wait."

Her shaky voice almost gave out. "OK."

"Maybe after you feel better I could tell a little about where I grew up to keep your mind busy. Just key the microphone back up when you feel ready," Bo offered. He preferred to keep his personal life to himself. If it helped Sally through a few hours behind a locked door then he could deal with it.

She started to do as he said, breathing slowly with her eyes closed. It took some time, but she did feel better, relaxed if not terribly uncomfortable lying on the metal gurney. Sally let him know she was doing better. She felt so worn out from the adrenaline rush the panic brought on. Without warning she dozed off.

* *

Power surged through her from the setting sun, waking her up abruptly. The vibrant influx of magic washed over Sally, covering her body in a blanket of energy. Her feelings ran rampant, from giddiness to elation at the return of power, finally in the end drawing up her lust. Bo had worked hard with her to contain that beast several nights in a row before she could rein it in. This time it struggled against her commands to bend to her will. She had enough of her wits to know the door to her drawer needed to stay closed until she locked down those desires. Sally grabbed the walkie-talkie hoping the other end wasn't turned off yet. With a sigh of relief, he answered back. After she rapidly pleaded for her door to stay shut a banging on her door came back as his reply. She had forgotten to release the talk button.

It took a few minutes before feeling she could have one of them to unlock her door. At the same time Sally regained control, the door swung open bringing with it a flood of light and sound. Bo stood there talking to Dirk as her door opened. It didn't matter so long as her lust stayed under control and she was out of that confounded drawer. It felt so good to stretch her limbs out once more that she did not notice the other sounds around her at first.

Banging drew everyone's attention to a neighboring drawer from the one Sally slept in. She, Bo, and Dirk went to the ominous noise, dumbfounded by what could be causing it. More cadaver drawers produced the same banging noises as the first, getting louder by the minute. Bo said he hadn't seen or felt anything mystical the whole time they waited, and his sight didn't show any rituals here.

With little choice left to them, they each took a drawer to open, not knowing what to expect, and pulled the latches at the same time. Muffled sounds became screams of rage and panic as dead bodies from the drawers pushed their way out. Not a one of the dead said anything that Sally could understand, just moaning in place while they struggle to stand.

"Dirk, get her somewhere safe! I'll hold them off for as long as I can. Now move!" Bo yelled over his shoulder, already throwing up his hands to cast out some sort of spell.

Dirk dragged Sally down the hall to some elevators, the echoes of fighting following them. He franticly pressed the call button as if it would bring the elevator faster. The doors opened and they jumped in; Dirk relaxed slightly as the elevator started its way up to the next floor. When the doors opened, he guided her with a purpose down a hallway, determined to get as far away as he could from the horror movie scene happening back there.

Dirk led her to a cafeteria where Sally would not look out of place standing around. He seemed to have gotten some of his composure back after the initial fright and followed her to a drinking fountain while she tried to eliminate a dry mouth brought on by her fear; apparently he needed to do the same.

When Dirk finished up he gave her a few dollars, waving at the distraught cashier demanding payment. "I need to go back to help out. Please stay here until we get back. There might not be anything I can do for him, but I need to make sure he got out."

Not know what else to do with herself as she watched him head off, Sally walked over to stand behind people already in line for food. She needed a cup of coffee badly to help steady her. It was either that or pacing back and forth bringing undue attention. Coffee seemed the wisest choice.

Before she could finish the piping hot cup of coffee, Dirk had returned with Bo. Their heads were close together speaking in hushed tones to keep others from hearing them, puzzlement clearly evident on both their faces. They sat down at her table without another word said between them. Sally could tell something was not right about the whole thing. Bo's reaction along with snippets of their conversation she did hear bounced around in her head; visit the shaman, Larry will know what to do, and something about being the wrong time for undead to rise. Bo looked as if he had seen a ghost sitting there—almost white to the bone. It scared her to see him, a man who had been around a long time, look as terrified as he did right now.

"The dead just don't get up. It's unheard of. They acted like zombies without uttering a word, just groaning the whole time." Bo stared out to nothing as he went on, "I did what I could with shields and other spells, but it had little effect on them. They wouldn't stop coming."

"How'd you get away then?" she asked baffled.

"They all dropped to the floor, all at once. First they rise up then they fall down." Bo seemed to be babbling now. Nervousness bled off of him in sheets.

Sally wanted to help him focus. "Did you feel any change when they dropped? Anything different happen after we left?"

"Nothing I could see," Bo replied coming back to the here and now. "Nothing besides you two leaving."

Clearly bothered from the experience, Bo looked back the way he came in saying, "We'll leave the hospital soon, after we make sure those dead people stay that way. I need better answers than I'll get sitting here. Dirk's going to need help cleaning up before someone finds them lying all over the floor."

"Yeah, I don't know how I'd explain that one away," Dirk said, chuckling at the thought.

Bo stood up suddenly and strode out of the cafeteria not looking back. Sally was beginning to find it irritating the way he expected others to just follow, but she didn't see any other way than following him with Dirk in tow. They put the morgue back in order before anyone noticed the mess, saying their good-byes quickly. Soon enough they were back on the road heading under the cover of night to a camp of undead.

Boy, this should be even more fun, Sally said to herself, dreading the idea of meeting kindred spirits.

CHAPTER 13

Forbidding enveloped her as they drove through the mountain pass. Flashes from her recent past haunted Sally, giving her reason to worry a tire might burst and send them over the edge. Luck didn't seem to be on their side at the moment the way things have gone. What bothered her most was the dream she'd had. The surrounding trees closed in on her with each passing mile messing with her head. Sally wrapped arms around her body, attempting to abolish an oncoming feeling of skin being ripped from her body wishing she didn't remember that from the dream. The ride up put her in a miserable mood.

Their destination sat in a place south of Aspen, Colorado, in the deeper part of the forest among hiking trails. Bo turned off the paved road following one of the many dirt roads to a trailhead. A few cars were parked with their occupants already on hikes through nature. He pulled up to the service road entrance, grabbing a ring of keys from the glove box before getting out. Sally sat there in the car while he unlocked the padlock. Feeling the ominous trees staring back at her, she closed her eyes in a vain effort to calm her racing heart with the breathing technique Bo had had her do back at the morgue.

The click of the door handle gave Sally a start as he got back in the car. Bo looked at her questioningly; she just shook her head without saying anything so Bo had the good graces not to say anything either. They drove to the other side of the entrance for Bo to secure its chain back keeping unwanted visitors out.

Turning to watch him lock the door kept Sally's mind on the mundane movements it took to secure the chain. She could almost swear she heard the lock click into place just before a flare of light momentarily blinded her. She threw her hands up to deflect the source of instant pain in her head. It only lasted seconds, but now throbbing beat ceaselessly inside of her head. When she could see straight again, Sally forced out the words slowly to ask what happened.

Bo turned to her, bemused as to why she would ask such a question. "I just locked the entrance is all. What are blinking like that for? Did some of the dirt come through the vent, or are you going to start crying because you're so pleased I came back?" He finished with a smirk she wanted to smack off his face.

"Because of that flash, you idiot! Just after you locked up the gate it hit me," Sally said, still wiping the pain from her eyes.

"What flash?"

Sally began to get distressed. "At first I thought it was my head that hurt after being hit by the brilliant light, but it was my eyes that continued hurting when the pain subsided from my head. The flash caused it. Now tell me what I saw," she said, angry and hurt all at once.

Understanding dawned on his face. "Oh, the boundary wards. It's been so long since I even paid any mind to the protection put on the chain. I can't say why you saw it that way though; I only see a dull ping of half-light when the lock is reengaged. The protection is there to discourage hikers from taking this road." He thought a little more on what she said before replying, "Could just be how new you are at being dead and the magic in you formed a keener sight for such things. I can only guess, but it is one more thing we can ask my guy when we get there. The shaman's not too far from here.

"By the way, before my absentmindedness seems to prevail I should tell you more boundaries are out here. They divide territories between supernatural species out there."

Just up from the entrance and around a meandering curve, Sally noticed the trees fairly spread out but getting closer. The forest ahead was nearly impenetrable with the naked eye. Sally watched the thick scenery passing by, a rabbit caught her attention as it bounced back into the brush. When she brought herself back facing forward, fog as think as pea soup masked the road ahead. She hadn't seen fog a moment ago.

Sally scarcely saw any trees marking the dirt path Bo used for a road. Within the fog shapes appeared to dart back and forth across the road. Bo placed a hand on her leg to calm her apparent fear; had it been any other time she would have batted it away. Not right now, though.

No, right now the only thing keeping her from pulling on the wheel was the fact Bo knew the area and had a better idea of the danger this trip carried. She settled back down and he removed his hand, which relieved her all the more.

Suddenly a figure stood just visible beyond the mist in the middle of the road. Sally couldn't help but wonder if a hiker had gotten lost in the fog. Concerned for the person's safety after seeing the darting shadows in the woods, she turned to Bo. He was grunting under his breath muttering, "Idiots."

He had already spotted the figure standing in the way and from his reaction recognized the silhouette. They were passing through the supernatural territories he told her about. *After what Bo told me on the ride up, you would think there was a make-believe service road to travel safely. The borders should have been worked out better if this stuff always happened,* she pondered.

* *

Bo did need this delay because of some jerk with a beef against everything and anyone. He burned with outrage at the way these guys thought they had rights to everything. *We are the ones that made this whole thing possible in the first place. What, with undead taking up positions in congress and wildlife preservation groups to secure the land as a preserve, to even keep out the strip mining companies creating the perfect privacy.*

This one ahead was going to be trouble, he thought to himself in resignation of what would come. Pulling to a stop in front of the shadowy figure, Bocnic shut off the engine and prepared to get out. "Stay in the car," he demanded of Sally. He didn't wait for a rebuttal.

She went to speak anyway and he gestured her silent, which she obeyed but not on her own. He had cast a simple spell to silence her against her will. He did not feel right doing it, but it was necessary if they were going to get out of this one in one piece. Stepping out of the car took effort, as he did not want to deal with this at the moment.

The figure posing as a blockade went by the name Karton. He'd had a chip on his shoulder ever since they went head-to-head some years back. Werewolves tended to forget about clothes because it just got in the way of transformations, so Karton stood naked before him.

"You know passage through our lands demands payment." Karton spoke with a commanding tone.

"That was yesterday," Bocnic replied nonchalantly. "Besides, the dispute for payment ended long ago with the agreement between clans for free passage to and from the main road."

"I didn't agree. Pay or fight for your right."

"You know how this will end. Just like the last time we…" Before Bo could finish the sentence, he was body slammed against the car's hood.

From the corner of his eye Bo saw Sally crouch away from the windshield, afraid it might cave in. He forced his knees between them when his opponent rose to get a better position over him. With the leverage he gained Bo rolled off the car to the ground and found himself on top. Breaking the grip on his shoulders, he jumped away using Karton's stomach as a launch pad. Bo somersaulted through the air as he watched Karton transform to his natural form of a wolflike human. Amazed still at the speed with which these creatures could flip from one form to the other, Bo touched lightly back to the ground some yards away. Distance mattered little to werewolves with their massive leg muscles. Not given much time to prepare, Bo crossed his arms at the wrists, bringing up a flimsy shield, bending at the knees to ward off the freight train about to hit him. Dirt rose up and over his feet as an anchor at the last second before he felt the full force of the charge; the hardened dirt around his ankles held him steadfast.

Air he didn't know he was holding passed lips from the impact of the blow. Karton deflected off the shield up into the branches of a nearby tree and ricocheted to the ground below with a sickening crack as he landed headfirst. The flimsy shield Bo had mustered could absorb any force taken and return it twofold back on the opponent. A trick he had used on this werewolf before, though Karton seemed to have forgotten. Deafening cracks came from the tree as dead branches rained down on Karton from the impact. The werewolf picked himself up, shaking off the bark, and spittle of blood flung from his mouth as well as blood trickling down from his wounded collarbone.

Pain enraged the werewolf, giving him strength to overcome the mangled shoulder. With an inhuman scream sounding, much like a howl, Karton charged from a greater distance attempting to take Bo down. Before the wolf crossed halfway, he used his snout as a scoop tossing dirt at the shield, revealing a hole near Bo's knees. With a grin Karton dove for the gap and grabbed his legs at the calves, causing the shield to disintegrate and sent them both cartwheeling into the brush.

Bo screamed out in pain as Karton bit down on his ankle, blood spilling as the foot separated from the leg. Spitting the foot under the car, Karton turned back to his prey with claws raised as Bo sideswiped the beast's head with magic encasing his fist for good measure, connected directly with the lower jaw. Karton was momentarily stunned by the blow, and Bo grappled him to the ground, straddling him. Another punch with a rushed chant aimed at the other shoulder smashed into it so hard he felt ground beneath, drawing a panicked scream from Karton.

Standing over the crippled werewolf, he effectively held him down with the jagged edge of bone left from his missing foot held at Karton's throat. "That's enough," Bo announced, breathing a little heavily, strained to the point of exhaustion. "Take your pack and move out. This stays between us unless you push it and I'm forced to inform the council. Do we see eye to…foot?"

"Done," Karton said pushing away from Bo with only his legs. The damage done to his shoulders would heal in an hour or so. The pack stood by waiting for their leader to recover by himself. Karton would have to face his pack of wolves injured in order to regain leadership over them again. Bo did not care.

CHAPTER 14

Sally had been watching from the passenger seat the whole time with her mouth wide open; now it was as dry as the desert. Bo moved with such grace that she was in awe of it. She'd heard most of the conversation by cracking the window to hear them better. Some of it was clear enough to understand, but all that talk about boundaries and deals seemed out of place.

Leaning on the car, Bo reached under it to retrieve his severed foot. He got back into the car, slumping in the seat. He held the foot in his hand and crossed his legs to bring the mangled leg in sight. Putting the two pieces close together brought a burning red glow around them, stretching skin to seal with its counterpart. Bo cringed, suffering through the pain of regrowth. Sally remembered all too clearly of her own ordeal and how it felt. Light faded when the two became one, toes wiggling to test the connection. Feeling he had put it back right, Bo swung around in the seat and put the car in gear without another word.

They watched the wolves run off in the opposite direction of the camp. Only then did Bo say it was safe to move on. As they drove away from the devastation brought on by the fight, Sally looked back to see the glares from the remaining pack as they melded back into the forest. They sat in silence for the rest of the trip watching the surrounding landscape shift between pine, aspen, and other various shrubs. Both watched precariously for anything else to jump out of the ominous fog.

It appeared that the camp was ahead when Bo started up conversation again. She had forgotten his spell put on her earlier until she couldn't ask a question. Sally slapped him on the shoulder to get Bo's attention, gesturing to her mouth before he understood the problem. Bo shrunk back in his seat ashamed for neglecting such a small detail. Once he made everything right again he mentioned stuff about what to expect and not to be surprised at some of the oddities she might witness. *I can't believe some of the things Bo's saying, but he says it with such concerned sentiment.* She chided herself, *I have to get over being so skeptical of everything.*

However, it seemed she had seen some of the undead before, although maybe not in person. "Are you good with your history and not just political either?" he asked. "Maybe Elvis?"

Sally raised her eyebrows as she listened. "You're kidding, he's undead? So the sightings are real and he does it to raise the dander of the fans?"

"Some get a kick out of their fifteen minutes under the spotlight even if it is decades past their prime."

Sally couldn't help herself from laughing about dead people having fans. Sobering up to a better mood, she had to ask about the spat Bo just hobbled away from—if he was dead, why the weakness act? To her surprise he answered more quickly than in the past.

Bo fell into a storyteller's voice as he retold the history of this land and what the beef with Karton was about. "The fatigue I experienced after the fight came from blatant overuse of my magic. Magic in all forms takes its penance one way or another. Also, one other thing to keep in mind I didn't tell you is that I still have to breathe now and again for my flesh looking alive and to talk. The muscles still need oxygen to function, too. Normally, what I did back there wouldn't have been a difficult task, still ready for more fighting. I miscalculated how much magic I needed for the shield and you saw what it did to Karton.

"I had to use a mix of physical and mental magic for me to win and by doing so caused my body to act like a car's engine running on fumes. Go any harder and the tank is empty, stranded. Time is the only way to heal from any depletion of magic, and until then the body will deteriorate slowly until the magical batteries can recharge or I can get my hands on an undead elixir duly named 'Deadman's drink' to kick-start the process. The drink's name is moronic, I know, but sometimes it is easier to keep it simple than use some mystic name no one can pronounce."

Driving on down the dirt path another brilliant flash of light temporarily blinded Sally again sitting helplessly unprepared. She brought her head to rest in the crook of her arm to fend off the light grenade. Bo glanced over to see what was wrong after a stifled scream emitted, then realized what had happened.

"Welcome to the dead lands. Sorry for not warning you about the second boarder wards. They were set up for each of the lands to deter each species of supernatural from crossing accidentally into a rival's place and setting off a war, although some cross over on purpose to incite the other group," Bo said offhandedly to keep her mind off the sightless pain.

Entering the camp he parked the car under a camouflaged tent with the other cars. Sally got out of the car to be hit by the night's cold breeze as some of the camp locals came walking up. A few Sally recognized on sight, but most didn't have any resemblance to anyone famous. And of all people, Elvis walked by with a quick wave and a quicker exit. *Must still be in the "no autograph" phase at seeing a new face show up*, she thought. *A bit conceited.*

Sally noticed in the darkness of torchlight around the camp some of the undead moving about with missing parts like a foot, hand, and sometimes more. Bo schooled her in a whisper voice that if something was missing before the magic first started, it was always going to be missing, a fact of life and even in death.

"Where's Larry? He's around tonight I hope," Bo asked of the crowd standing nearby.

One of the unknown locals spoke up, "He's at his temple reciting some arcane ritual. To tell the truth, I think he's mumbling nonsense like usual and nothing is sure to come of it. I believe it's a good time to bother him."

"If things happen like the last time, you're helping to dig him out *and* make a new one," Bo retorted. "I am not going to be responsible if he blows this one up, too."

A hearty laugh came from the group as they walked off.

"What do you mean dig him out?" Sally asked, bewildered. "I see a few places here that look enough like houses to be for someone as prominent as this Larry guy to use."

"Oh, those are for 'newbies' that don't feel comfortable in the underground spaces made to hide our presence from any flyovers. I'll find out which one might be empty for you to sleep in while we're still here. He's over there," Bo said as they moved through the camp toward a large pile of dirt reminiscent of an Incan burial site Sally had seen on the History Channel.

Beneath a nearby grove of trees beyond the mound, she spotted a hole leading to the compartments below. As they crested the small hill next to the lip of the hole, she noticed steps leading down. A slightly bluish glow emitted around the rim with no other light source to speak of. Passing the rim of the entry, Sally felt a tingle run along her skin moving slowly past the entrance. She could not push away the nervous feeling that was building in her as she descended into the awaiting lair of the shaman, Larry. The only thing she could think of was that the name really didn't fit someone so powerful.

CHAPTER 15

The Chapel Hills Mall bustled with activity, and Rebecca found herself swept up in the shopping frenzy. It wasn't even Thanksgiving and yet the stores insisted on moving the pre-Christmas sale earlier and earlier every year. She tried to blame it on the recession, but Rebecca knew better. It was just another way to suck a customer in, and she was one of those to fall for it every time, if it meant saving a buck or two.

Filling both hands with her parcels and leaving her food tray behind for food court staff to clean up, Rebecca headed down the escalator to the front doors. It had gotten dark outside since she began the buying fiasco. Spending money really did take all day when little thought went into how much left her purse.

The parking lot had been partially full when she arrived, but now it was packed. The only thing she remembered was her car being near a middle section. Closing time for the mall grew near, yet a few people still headed in and fewer were coming out, looking for that last-minute deal. Proceeding through the sea of cars became a bit of a problem. All the bags hanging off her arms caught side mirrors or bounced off rear bumpers, putting her load off balance. A few bad attempts later under the parking garage lights brought her in sight of the little red car. Another mall shopper seemed to be in the same predicament of finding his car. He had a shopping bag in his hand, but she didn't want to take chances he might be something other than a shopper. Paranoid, that was all. Bag snatchers were known to wander the parking lots looking for an easy mark to take off with their packages; it had been all over the news as of late.

Ah, my little red Prius! she exclaimed triumphantly to herself over finding her car in such a short time, unlike the normal car hunting adventures she'd had. She moved with unfettered speed to the car, popping the trunk and stuffing her prizes into it. Sounds of gravel underfoot startled her as she closed the trunk. Rebecca pivoted to the sound as the man with a shopping bag behind her sent the sting of a taser gun roaring through her side. She wilted into the assailant's arms before passing out as headlights rounded the corner. She prayed the person in the van saw what happened.

She woke strapped to a military-style cot by the feel of it, with a blindfold across her eyes. Groggy from more than a shock from the taser, she didn't scream out right away. *They must have drugged me after taser to feel like this.* Panic taking over her thoughts. Rebecca could still feel her clothes had been untouched; it was a mild relief, but not much. She felt an engine rumble beneath the cot, realizing the vehicle was in motion.

Rebecca realized the vehicle had to be bigger than a car if she was lying down, bringing her to the notion that the van in the parking lot she spotted before passing out must have been the getaway van. The energy to yell flooded her, and Rebecca blasted out as loud as she could with a glass shattering scream. However, all she heard were chuckles from the men in the van.

"We're too far away for anyone to hear you. Might as well shut your yap before I help you," her capturer said flatly. He continued, evidently to the driver, "How far?"

"Should've been paying attention instead of staring at her. You know that's not going to happen anyway, so get your mind in the game. Anyways, we're just minutes away now," the driver retorted.

The van came to a rolling stop, a door slid open that could only be the panel door, and hands near her body lifting the cot made her gather strength to scream again. Her mouth opened to let loose, but she was dropped on her side before she could call for help.

"Shit!" yelled from one of the carriers while the sting of the electricity ran through her again. The stabbing prick in her arm made her drowsy, confirming they had drugged her again.

Waking with a splitting headache this time, Rebecca kept quiet while she tried to figure out what these new surroundings offered. She did not want another slam of voltage for merely whimpering. Her hand was outstretched, clamped to a table by the feel of the hard surface, sitting with the blindfold still in place. What made her nervous was how the cold metal bound her left hand to the wooden table with her fingers stretched apart. Rebecca heard a grunt followed by feet shuffling across the floor moving in her direction just before a searing pain shot through her arm and her heart-wrenching screech echoed off walls.

A fierce pain bloomed at the end of her hand, hot liquid running under her palm. Rebecca struggled to keep conscious from the pain radiating up her arm as she attempted again to pull her hand free. She felt a throbbing on the right side of her hand where the thumb would be when she noticed her thumb couldn't feel the table; she didn't feel *her* thumb.

Again she screamed out in agonizing pain both from the fresh cut and the rage of losing a finger. God only knew what else she would lose or endure. Was she captured by cannibals? *An irrational thought at a time like this*, she berated herself as speculating overcame panic of what was to come. Jabbing at the open wound stung her terrified thoughts outward again.

One of the men said, "Not reconnecting back."

Through her whimpering Rebecca heard the other say, "Dump her," as if this happen every day.

A new person entered her nightmare, a woman's voice this time, that said, "Pick a different place this time. Need to shake up things a little." Surprise could not cover what Rebecca felt at that moment, and the pain from her hand was forgotten, but only briefly.

Something hot passed by her shoulder down to her wrist before the female spoke again, "Just get it over with. She's not the one and we have more to track."

Burning overtook any other pain she felt in her body. Smoke trails carried to Rebecca's nose the smell of fried flesh, making her shake the chair violently in an effort to break it apart and escape. Her throat had become raw from repeated screaming, but it didn't matter as she once again passed out, this time from the sheer pain of torture.

CHAPTER 16

Leaving the darkness of the dug out stairwell behind them, they entered an anteroom with simple, smoothed dirt walls with an arched doorway. Moonlight filtered down the hole giving the room an appearance of a spotlight shining down on them. The angle of the hole bothered Sally. It was almost flush with the ground above without any sign of a door to close. Where did all the water go when it rained?

She remembered the prickly film of faint light over the hole, not sure how it could keep out water being see-through. The question dug at her until she turned to Bocnic to ask if it worked the same way his shield did to stay dry.

He replied, "Simply put, a shield can be made to do anything; the trick is knowing what to use, when. Larry probably had something up there, most likely a talisman, buried in the dirt nearby to keep the shield going without standing there to maintain it. Think of it like the boundary wards we passed through. Nothing to worry yourself over."

The anteroom gave way to a space filled with a few tables, bookshelves, an odd assortment of lanterns glowing naturally, and stacks of books either too big to fit on the bookshelves or had never been put back. Sounds of murmuring drifted out from the adjacent room as the shaman evoked some kind of magic spell with a repetitive chant. Beams of brilliant green light began to glow outward, blotting out the color in the room, then flicker and fade. Loud grumbling came shortly after in a language Sally didn't recognize. The shaman entered through the connecting doorway with his hands to his face, dropping them as Bo cleared his throat to draw attention their way.

Shock quickly vanished into recognition on the shaman's face; he faced Sally as if she might attack. Surprised by the shaman's attitude towards her, Bo quickly tried to make introductions, "Larry, this is Sally Mer—"

Larry's hands swished the air almost too fast for her to see, and Sally's arms were pinned to her sides.

He started yelling at the top of his lungs, irate at Bo for bringing such evil into his home. Another wave of his hand brought a chair to and then under Sally while straps came from nowhere to secure her. Bound like she was gave her a front row seat of Bo steadily trying to calm Larry down from his rantings about some apocalypse coming. Finally convinced Sally couldn't move anywhere, Larry waved Bo's words away.

The shaman explained she had the same skill blaring from her aura as did the Slaver from a time long past.

"Because it is a natural skill in magic she cannot be stifled the same way learned skills can."

He looked blankly around the room caught in some kind of revelation known only to him. Larry shook off the bad memory with a wave of his hand and cleared his throat before going on, "Learned skills can be nullified by countering them, but this is a completely different problem to contend with. The only way to handle this is to leave her in a graveyard, buried and forgotten."

Bo got Larry to settle down only after the shaman had made sure Sally could not get up. Slipping on leather workman's gloves for protection, he added gold handcuffs to her restraints from his desk in the corner. Sally missed what came next, distracted by the effects the cuffs were having on her. A draining feeling came over her body in small increments until she felt so mundane to the point of never having had the magic at all. Strange memories from other people started flooding in from nowhere. Flashes of people bound in handcuffs made it clear where the invading thoughts came from. Any trials or tribulations of the wearers' past experiences must have been stored in the cuffs were attacking her brain. Sudden bursts of electrically charged memories and thought traveled along her spine made her shoot upright, head outstretched to the ceiling above, mouth open in a silent scream. Had the two men been paying any attention, they might have seen a faint flickers of white light engulf the retinas of her eyes, lasting only seconds.

The rampant roller coaster of emotions left behind by the onslaught of knowledge subsided as slowly as the draining of magic had earlier. Hours seemed to have passed as Sally was forced to re-live other people's lives; all the while the two men didn't so much as look in

Sally's direction. She fought to regain her senses still reeling from the experience. Listening to Bocnic and Larry squabble over a girl and what should be done with her next...did they say a girl?

She was going to be twenty-six years old forever and they were calling her a mere girl? *I don't care what age they were born, women like myself get pissed about being called a child*, she thought, anger stirring her into a renewed will to fight.

Struggling against the golden cuffs made little difference. They weren't going to budge. Even attempts to tip the chair failed. Most likely something the shaman had done with his magic to hold it in place. Giving up prematurely on escape forced her to notice another change coming over her: a deep emptiness welling up within her. She drew into herself attempting to escape the stark barrenness unfolding, *I did not feel this the first time cuff were put on me. What's happening?*

She hadn't had the magic around for very long; however, the emptiness she felt with it gone made her acutely aware of how much it was going to be part of her life from here out. Sitting in the chair, bound, gave her the ridiculous thought of being naked, bared to these men. The futility of it all became unbearable. Her mind was out of control as it conjured randomly obscure thoughts. Sally felt she was losing herself and her mind. The room seemed darker, and the old pains from her recent car escape some days back returned, throbbing aches rattled all over her body. She realized the gold was drawing out almost all of the magical essence this time around. Without the healing properties from the magic to sustain her, Sally's body would dwindle back to being dead. She was almost convinced of it and it scared her.

Sounds of whimpering started filling the room with a hauntingly high pitch noise, rebounding off the hardened dirt walls before she become aware of where it actually came from... her own parched throat. Any motion or sound in the room stopped immediately around her as she wailed from the top of her lungs again at the anguish her body was being put through. Concern etched across Larry's face when he heard her, bringing him out of his triad of arguments about binding her. He quickly moved to her side to do what he could. Larry being so close brought Sally out of her self-loathing misery and silenced her.

He removed the worn gloves to bare his skin and placed his right hand on her forehead with his eyes closed, he began to chant something foreign while she watched him. The other hand he placed between her shoulder and left breast, bringing a reflexive protest from her lips, but Bo quieted her with a look that said he wasn't going to feel her up. She relaxed then to let the shaman do his work. Larry rotated his hand from forehead to leg, grimacing as if it were painful each time a hand moved to a different location.

Sally hadn't noticed until now that what was going on had distracted her enough to stop her worrying over the empty feeling a moment ago, and she was glad to have something else she could focus on instead of the turmoil inside. The chanting ceased before she knew it, and Larry stood up again from his inspection. Bo's words must have gotten through to him when Larry finally said, "Maybe she could be released for the time being," he said to no one in particular, "since she poses no real threat—yet."

Going back to his desk to open a drawer the cuffs had been kept in, he pulled the work gloves back on to remove a set of golden keys and unlock her restraints. When the handcuffs came off everything happened at once. It might as well have been floodgates the way her magic came rushing back to her. Sally's vision blurred as faint streaks of light surrounded her body a few feet off her skin and slowly closed in on her. The shaman stepped back from Sally and away from the abundant light, fear in his eyes from the spectacle before him. A vortex of magical energy swirled to her center like a planet collapsing in on itself. The dirt constructed room grew pitch black as the magic circled around her, snuffing out any of the magic sustaining the candles. Loose pages scattered around the room lifted off the ground to join the whirlwind.

Then in a blink of an eye it stopped. Magic slowly seeped back into the candles brightening it to reveal a room in a cluttered disarray, more than when they arrived.

"Holy crap, that was a ride," Sally squeaked out, sitting back up in her chair, muscles shaking to keep her upright, and breathing hard. They all were breathing as if they had run a marathon; Bo and Larry from the magic being retched from their bodies, and Sally giving over to the pure ecstasy her magic brought. Momentarily forgetting the straps still held her tightly in place.

The thoughts in her head now were not all her own anymore. Bits and pieces of other peoples' memories were lodged with her own. Casting images from other peoples' past pertaining to magic and of their everyday lives. It was almost like being in the middle of a babbling group of people where not one conversation stood out. When the voices in her head subsided, she could focus again on what was going on around her; both of the men were staring at her again. Sally looked down at herself checking just in case if the illusion earlier of being naked might be true before glancing back to give a stern look.

Larry had gone from being manic about the world ending to looking amused. Sally sat there confused at everything, thinking it the best course of action for the moment while the shaman said, "There's a chance she won't be like the other. I'll work with you, Sally, to see to that. Any wavering and I go back to plan A."

Sally didn't remember hearing what plan A was, but she didn't like the sound of it.

With a shake of his head at the shaman, Bo conceded to the idea while kneeling down to check Sally's wrists; there were burns from the cuffs. She looked down to where he gazed and could only stare at the burn marks she did not feel on her wrists. Seeing Bo's concern made her want to ask if this always happened but did not remember any from the first encounter. She also wanted to tell Bo about the memories but thought better of it, at least while the mood-shifting shaman was in earshot. As far as she knew, she could trust Bo with what happened; however, for anyone else her lips were sealed. Sally tried to think of about something in her recent past to reclaim her own mind from the new residence these memories were trying to take up. Thinking of Larry's name made an easy target.

"Larry? For some reason that name doesn't fit you. I don't mean to be rude, but 'Larry the magic doer' makes me want to giggle more than hide in terror," Sally said with a smirk. "I'm not forgetting what you did to me a moment ago, which hurt, but I would have expected a more ominous name for a person like you."

"Tutin'ru-mal is my real name from when I was born back in Egypt in the almost forgotten age of the pharaohs. Too hard to pronounce for most, so I came up with an easier name fitting the times. I like it," the shaman proclaimed proudly, "Now, let me take a closer look at you."

Larry circled her, looking at her from head to toe with grunts and mumblings about something not being right with her aura. She watched him as he backed away to sit at the desk chair against the far wall. The shaman rubbed his chin in consideration over her aura, scratching his head. In the end, he only said Sally's aura was an ever-changing landscape. "It might be a side effect of you being such a young undead or it could be something else. I'm not sure, but I think I've seen it before."

Larry allowed her move around the room if she wanted to, as long as she touched nothing. That did not sit well with Sally, but she let it slide for now. She walked in the opposite direction to get herself some breathing room away from Larry and gather her thoughts. Come to think of it, she did have more control now without some other person's thoughts overriding her own. Footsteps let Sally know Bo had walked off with Larry into the only other room from where the chanting first emitted.

Taking a better look around, she couldn't help but see the fine layers of dirt covering everything in the room after the escapade her tumultuous of magic had caused. Closer inspection of the room showed the walls had a smooth finish, appearing almost glossy and helped the flickering candle light stretch further into the room. Candles stood in floor stands burning brightly again - now that magic was restored - without putting off smoke trails, casting faint light but never reaching the darkest of corners. Besides the desk in the room there were a few tall bookshelves scattered about. Rafters and supporting beams of thick wood kept all the dirt from crashing in, possibly destroying Larry's collection.

"What's up with all the books? Haven't you been around long enough to memorize the whole collection by now?" Sally yelled out over the noise being stirred up in the next room. No answer came back.

Apprehensive to be in the same room as the shaman so soon, she held back from peeking in to see what they were doing. Saying it louder still came back without a response. Sally was concerned Larry might be a little too tightly wound at the moment, ready to spin on her at any moment if he saw her. She wasn't ready to risk another mood swing from him just yet, but the sounds of heavy furniture being moving around perked her curiosity enough to overcome the fear. Sally leaned around the door for a better look.

The room they were in matched the dirt floor in the first, but the walls and ceiling were covered in a variety of wood planks sealing away the packed dirt beneath it. *Every variety of tree had been used to fill the room*, she thought; making it feel like a large wooden box. Some kind of foreign writing was burned into the panels, she realized, in a language she did not know; oddly enough no pentagrams could be seen anywhere. She always thought magic had some kind of pagan symbolism related to it.

At her approach, a faint yellowish glimmering radiated out to her from the entryway. The radiating force of the doorway mildly pushed her back from going through. Still unused to being around magic, she refrained from pushing back at it and maybe causing it to blow up. Taking the safe road, Sally moved over to let Larry see her as she called out, "Am I that big of a problem you need to block yourselves in?"

"Oh, bother. It's something I worked up to keep my work from blowing another hole in the ground." He motioned to the writings on the walls. "Let me cross the entry to let you in."

After they all were in the same room, she got a better look at his workspace. A couple of tables had what looked like a mad scientist's chemistry set with multitudes of beakers in varying colors mixing and remixing liquids until finally dripping into some glass jars at the end. Bo held one of these jars filled with a splattering of Halloween colors swirling in it to his lips, sipping. Animal furs with a feral glow to them sat stacked in one corner. Sally only saw a few patterns in the furs of stripes like a zebra or others with black speckled spots not unlike a cheetah's that she could recognize in the furs, and she asked why Larry had need of furs if the dead didn't feel the cold.

Bocnic answered for the shaman since Larry seemed preoccupied with the arrangement of the tables. "The quick answer is that they are trophies from fights with different were-beasts. Some are from fights as a rite of passage, and others are from struggles for power between the undead and rival factions. Larry has only agreed to a fight if he's allowed to keep the pelt. The trick to getting a fur is skinning the were-animal before it changes. So the beast is beaten within an inch of it's life before he can skin it. Don't worry, he never kills the donor."

Sally felt sick to her stomach and tasted a little bile rise in the back of her throat. "Disgusting," was all she could muster.

"Slaughtering of animals for magic isn't a glamorous job. Probably why there aren't more mages as of late. A piece of scrap from just one pelt can generate enough power for a spell to equal the devastation of Hiroshima if it is condensed and refined enough. Simple chants or incantations do the job without the needed bloodshed to obtain a creature's skin. On the other hand, what Larry can prepare beforehand can obliterate any spoken spell," Bo said pointing to the array of bunsen burners and test tubes.

"It's a dying art that won't be missed. If you ask around most will tell you just that, but it has too many uses in my book for it to stick around," Bo concluded as Larry returned from his inner turmoil of room decorating.

Larry gestured her to have a seat on the stool. When she took her place he went across the room to one of the tables, rummaging through some of the items laying on its scarred top. She sat on the three-legged wooden stool, glancing back at the door, reluctant to sit down for this man again. Larry assured her that he wouldn't tie her up again "unless absolutely necessary," all the while grinning to himself. She could not tell if he was being serious or not and fidgeted in her seat trying to get comfortable in the meantime. Her shot nerves kept trembles running down her body making Sally grip the edges on the stool to hide that fact.

"The first thing you should have been taught was to hide your smell," he said in a professor's tone.

"I don't smell! True, it has been over a day since we were able to stop…"

Larry quickly interrupted her. "You're right about your not smelling, but I didn't mean your hygiene. This is something that happens to the undead because the magic has to perpetually sustain the body in its 'natural' state at all times. You might not like it, but your body is deteriorating nonetheless. Over time the smell will get stronger, and people will notice an odor when you are in a room, but might not want to comment. It's like a locker room floor that's been bleached time and again; however, the sweaty foot odor always prevails. It can become a far worse smell than that though.

"Here, let me demonstrate for you—" and as the shaman did she saw what looked like a sheer curtain appear around him in the shape of a sphere expanding around him, then drop to the floor.

The odor hit her faster than expected. Sally could not get far enough away from the fetid smell taking over the limited space. *Week-old spoiled milk smelled better*, Sally thought inwardly as she fought back a need to vomit. Her gag reflex was getting a workout today, and she fought to control it before her stomach went full steam. Another muted flash she caught from the corner of her sight took the smell away as fast as it had emerged; although some of it still lingered in the air.

"Sorry, it has been some time since I last dropped that veil. Have to remember to do it more often." Larry mused, seeming to talk to himself more than small group, red spreading across his face from embarrassment when he looked at them both.

"After you learn to do this trick it will become an afterthought, as I have clearly shown. It's time we practice some skills like this one. I need you to close your eyes for this...no, I am not going to do anything to you," he promised, irritated at her unspoken accusation.

"Now, imagine yourself standing with nothing else around – in a completely empty room. In that nothingness form a bubble around your body that is double the space you are tall. Good, I can feel the hum of magic beginning to form around you. Slowly shrink the bubble until it is almost touching the skin."

Sally could just make out the last of what he had said as the imaginary bubble closed in; a loud droning noise built up in her head, making outside noises too hard to hear. Much like flying in an airplane, the sound in her head built up pressure until it wound down with a sudden pop, as they would to in a plane. The spell had failed miserably. Her hearing returned just as quickly with a little ringing left behind to annoy her.

Larry grunted satisfaction as he walked away to look for something on one of his tables with the beakers, and Sally began to feel slightly dizzy; playing with magic must have put a drain on her metaphorical batteries. Her failed bubble mixed with being restrained by gold could explain away her sudden worn-down feeling – perhaps, and then again she really did not know the first thing about all of this. Now that she thought about it, a nap sounded good if there was a bed close by. Out of the two rooms she realized she never spotted a bed or a place for one. The shaman returned with a thick looking concoction of a brownish-orange color, placing it in her hands and motioning her to drink.

Lifting it to her nose, Sally could not define the smell other than it was slightly unwelcoming. Swallowing it was a completely different situation; the taste was not a taste but a flood of emotion. It felt more like an awakening if nothing else. It was the only way she could think someone might be able to put it into words. She didn't just feel herself becoming more alive but it rekindled all the memories transferred from the golden cuffs. The floodgates were open again from the hidden power within the drink; however, these intruding thoughts had less of a grip on her this time. She thought that had all been part of her imagination until now. The more she swallowed the less those abstract memories faded.

Sally felt compelled to finish the mixture without stopping until the beaker was completely drained. Handing the beaker back to Larry, she looked down at her hands and noticed the tremors she had been experiencing from her shot nerves were now steady as steel. With a quick thought she popped the bubble around her to hide the nonexistent smell she carried. It was effortless this time, and the shaman noticed it with a bit of astonishment flashing through his pearly blue eyes. "Must have been from the power boost the drink gave you," he grumbled. Sally figured he did that often.

A confidence seemed to come with the power boost she'd received, and she blurted out how the dead had jumped to their feet in the morgue and acting like zombies she had seen in movies. Sally had been nervous at the hospital when the dead tried to rise from their cold storage; how their falling silent after she left the morgue sort of made sense now. Larry sat back down to think over what she'd said, stroking his chin all the while. She seemed to notice he did that a lot, too.

He sat there for some time preoccupied until he burst out with, "Dark times are ahead. Her mere presence proves another uprising will come to pass. She will have control over anything dead including some of the younger undead, capable of enslaving the masses. The last one to have this kind of power only exploited it on the undead and for his sole benefit, but he could have had the ability such as she does to control all levels of undead including vampires."

Looking at Bocnic, the shaman unconsciously spoke in a lower voice, not trying to exclude Sally from the conversation. "She already knows there's a crossroads ahead to pick right from wrong. The choices made from here out will decide her fate, and I will stand behind her one hundred percent so long as she stays for the side of the undead. She works against us, then I will personally take her down." He glanced at Sally.

"Don't take my change of heart about you as weakness. I don't mean to threaten you into choosing the right way. I'm only letting you know the consequences." He turned back to Bo. "We'll help train her at this camp while she stays with you. Some of the others here can teach hand-to-hand while I will instruct her in magic personally." He thumbed her way. "She is going to need all the help we can give her if she wants to survive the Church or any other opposition out there."

Larry made to take a breath for more ranting before Sally broke in with her own statement. "I have had self-defense classes and some military background," she said with a smug look crossing her arms across her chest. "I was pretty good, too."

Laughing seemed to come from all directions at once as Sally looked to Bo then back to Larry. "What?" She felt her ire build up at their heckling.

Bo was the first to speak up. "Military is a good place to learn defensive measures if you actually go to a war, and self-defense can be helpful against regular people, but bayonet training isn't going to save you when Supers, a fond name we like to use for supernatural species out there, are your enemy. Some of the karate style moves will do some justice; however, we know a thing or two about combining fighting with magic. Did you already forget about Karton and his gang?"

Sally deflated at the memory of the fight.

Larry threw a suggestion out ignoring the werewolf's name, "Why don't you gather up some of the better fighters while I get started here teaching her a little more magic, since she is so apt at learning. I don't expect her to remember everything I teach her, but she has a knack for magic."

Sally looked to Bo, putting on her best puppy dog eyes, "Could I have a radio to work by? I can concentrate a lot better with a little background noise." Larry protested but she won out; the music would play only while she worked. She felt a strong connection to hear music at the moment that she couldn't shake.

CHAPTER 17

Demric was losing patience by the hour. Weeks had passed without the girl being found. Efforts to step up the operation by kidnapping women fitting the vague description gave the same results. The order he commanded for testing each woman was taken a little too literally by his men. Testing the captives ended up drawing the wrong kind of attention from local and state authorities, including the F.B.I. Without clear orders on how to test the girls, the team killed the first few of them. It seemed logical at the time for his men, since undead could not die. That's how they ended up front-page news.

Disgruntled at these turn of events led Demric to rephrasing his orders to have a single finger cut off. *The undead reattached parts all the time, so this might keep the heat off those working for him*, Demric thought. He believed this would also lead the manhunt for a serial killer away from them, though it didn't. *How much farther will this fall apart before we nab the wench?* he reluctantly questioned himself.

He had told his men to slow down on picking up candidates, thinking the police would get lost in all the paperwork and red tape along the way. In the past week his men had cut down on how many they gathered up and spreading out the pickup points, throwing everyone off the scent for now. Something needed to give before he was forced to extract the team from Colorado all together. At this point failure could not rear its ugly head any farther or his superiors might have his own head.

They were hounding him for results with hopes that more than just the girl would be found. They wanted to eradicate a whole camp. It had been too long since the last raid, at least a century ago, and bloodthirstiness showed in their collective eyes from the latest meeting he had in their presence. More than anything they wanted results, and so did he. Bothered by the whole mess, he busied himself with the never-ending backlog of paperwork piling up on his desk.

The phone rang.

The button on the business phone lighting up was not the usual one dedicated for the inner office calls. This was one phone number specifically for informants. It had stunned him so to see it blink that he almost missed picking up the receiver before the last ring. "Hello," he said relaxing his voice to keep the person from knowing his nerves were shot. And the voice on the other end raised his spirits more.

Mike had finally called. "The grapevine is active about a girl you might be looking for. I heard about the kidnappings and figured it to be some of your men floating around my town causing havoc with the locals. Mathyas is a little pissed about that, too," Michal relayed with a bit of disgust underlying his words apparently aimed at his own leaders if not at the Church sniffing around Colorado.

Using the tracking software on the computer to pinpoint Mike's location was worthless since he only used throwaway phones when he called and these undead seemed to have a knack at hacking cell towers to hide the locations anyway. Ecstatic from getting this call could not begin to cover how Demric felt; however, he hid it the best way he knew how by throwing angry words around. "Who is she? Why did you wait to call if you knew we were down there? What's taking you so long to answer, damn it!"

Perturbed at the rapid firing of questions, Michal delayed answering right away; Demric should have taken a slower approach to coddle the bastard. *There still are ways to draw out the bits that matter most*, Demric said to himself, knowing the outpouring of words had let Michal get a glimmer of his current state of mind. He concealed it the best way he could by saying, "Michal, my outburst was unwarranted. I apologize for that, but what can you tell me that I already don't know?"

"She raises the dead."

Nothing would come out of Demric's mouth. He had never heard of such a thing in all the time he had been working for the Church. "What do you mean 'raise the dead'? That's an oxymoronic statement if I've ever heard one," he spat with distaste coating each word.

"You don't get it. She can raise dead that were never meant to come back to life. As far as a name to give her, that didn't come with the report Mathyas got. He was told a girl near Denver could do this and that she was getting some local training from some undead. That and his decision to physically take her apart to prevent her from dominating the world of the undead," Michal said matter-a-factly.

There was a minor pause before he concluded with, "Mathyas is scared of her."

"Good job, Mike. Please keep in touch with anything else that comes your way, and we can see to your payment in the near future," Demric said and hung up before Mike could protest the timing of the payment. Michal wanted to truly die, and the Church had made the illusion of being able to help him reach that goal believable. If Mike or any other undead wanted to offer intelligence on movements of any supernatural activity, then the Church would make up any tale to gain an advantage in their ongoing fight against such dark creatures. Such a shallow promise really, and that was why he had the closet of undead parts near his office. All of the spies for the Church had to receive payment at some point; it just wasn't what they expected. Such a win-win situation the Church had formed.

Forgetting protocols, he picked up the phone in his haste to share the news. Demric didn't see himself as a person looking for praise for a job well done, but he would make an exception this once by making the call. Removing the receiver from its cradle and placing it in the crook of his neck, he floated a finger over the red button, a direct line to his highest superior. He wanted to compose himself before pressing the button, knowing the outrage he would get for disturbing them. He pushed the button anyway once he was ready.

"This better be worth your head to bother me," a gravelly voice replied.

"It's Demric, I have news of the girl," he blurted out without thinking. *So much for composure*, he scolded himself.

"I know who this is you imbecile. What news is worth my time if it isn't about her being transported here?" the voice demanded on the other end.

He smiled briefly over his next words, shrugging off the superior's lack of understanding, "My informant just checked in. The new symbols the Temerdon pointed out make sense now. She raises the dead." Those symbols on the Temerdon that glowed had bothered him when no prior alert to a rising had even been pointed out in the past. He wrote a note to record the event for any future risings for himself.

"A Bringer is born!" Coughing ensued briefly from the outburst before his superior could continue, "We need to do everything in our power to bring her in. Don't screw this one up."

Demric clenched fists on his desk, resisting the urge to pound them. He was enraged at how they thought he would screw everything up when he had never failed them before. Looking for the calm within him, he asked, "What is a Bringer? Nothing I have down here mentions such a thing."

Sounds of distain wafted through the connection clearly enough to make Demric's blood pressure rise again. "It's a secret kept under lock and key for good reason. You will not share this information with anyone or we will be feeding the new tree we plant above you on Arbor's Day.

"She is only the second of her kind to have power over anything undead. Having her in our grasp could do wonders for the Church. Early Hebrew writings talked of a man enslaving dead to work for the Egyptians, but we never found his remains after they defeated him. The Church removed any information about this from the public eye and stored it away for safe keeping."

Demric doubted the Church was the real winner if they caught her. It sounded more like they would use her as a puppet for their own ends under the Church's name. He didn't have a problem with that, just the means they might use to make it so. Apparently this had been the goal of the Church when the written histories were first found. They must have given up chase long ago trying to find the remains of the first Bringer, since his department wasn't being involved with a continued search and he knew nothing about it.

Brushing off the earlier stab to his performance, he spoke up with what he considered an ace in the hole. "There is one more thing my informant passed on." He paused for dramatic effect. "Civil unrest flows in the ranks of the undead. The chief of the western clans is scared. It sounds as though he and some of his kind want to undo her before she can learn to use her power."

Laughter echoed down the receiver. "This is good news. If she is feeling ousted by her own kind, we may have a chance to sway her yet." The speaker dropped his tone a few notches before he continued, "We still are not satisfied with the progress made so far. Your men are being sloppy. This news you bring, albeit good, does not sway the other members from wanting to replace you. If you fail in this I will see to it you are." He hung up.

Demric fumed. So be it. Any longer on the phone and he might have said the wrong thing. He remembered the scribbled note he'd made about symbols, tore it up, and put it with the rest of his burn papers for later.

They were outraged that she was not in the Church's grasp yet and clearly didn't want to be bothered again until that happened. He knew it was the same ploy he himself had used on Mike to spur the spy into collecting more information. A new plan formed as he picked the receiver up. Placing a call to his men, Demric told them to regroup for an assault on the camp. He left it short and to the point as his men in command insisted on. He would give the location when they gathered in one place.

The implications of having a power such as hers for the Church was astronomical in moving God's word forward compared to moving house to house "saving" people from sin. It was one thing to teach the populous to fear a loving God but quite another to show them why they should fear him. Demric would need to gather his troops together in Colorado Springs, Colorado, for a do or die pep talk in capturing the girl.

He would not accept any kind of failure from them. Demric had to inform the heads of his own department locally, making clear his motives of redoubling the effort to snare this girl for the betterment of the Church. Not such a hard sell to his superiors, as plans went. He daydreamed the rest of the day about having the girl on a golden leash. She would have thousands of undead surrounding the benevolent hierarchy he worked for. They would cower from the power he welded at the leashes end. It made for a good afternoon.

CHAPTER 18

"She sure is a natural at this!" Don screamed over the chaos ensuing on the open practice area.

Sally's instructor turned back to the action, ignoring Bo for the moment as she threw a red lance of light at him. He tried to sidestep the shot and caught the brunt of the glowing lance in the shoulder, cleanly removing it from his body. Picking up his arm he hollered back to keep the fighting in the ring.

Bo knew standing this close to the field could be dangerous when Sally focused on too many targets at once. Her instructions had been to take out as many of them as she could without killing any. Her first lesson had been the platinum rule: don't kill unless there is no other option. When she questioned why not the "golden rule," there were snickers rampant in the crowd at such an absurd question. She must be taking her vengeance out on them now.

Sally had been working nonstop for weeks in an effort to learn all she could from the shaman and the others. The enhanced strength and speed Sally had gained from becoming undead took less time to master than others he had watched over. She surprised Larry with a couple of tricks he still did not know how she pulled off and still others that she helped him improve on. *Hard to imagine her teaching the teacher so soon*, Bo recanted.

During the previous weeks, Sally had been reluctant to open up about certain things that had happened to her after the handcuffs were put on. Testing the waters, she told him about the need for music to be around. It didn't bother her as much as it bothered Larry to constantly hear songs when he taught her magic. On one occasion the transmission broke up briefly in the middle of a song, neither thought anything of it. After a few more times, she wondered why the volume jumped up then settled back down. It had happened right before the chemistry set in front of Larry blew up. From then on Larry listen to the points Sally noted when the change in the signal happened. He figured the music she heard was a form of premonition and might manifest in other ways.

Once she felt comfortable telling him little secrets, she gave him her biggest one. In the end she told Larry about the foreign memories floating around her head. He thought it might be why she was such a good student, understanding the magic without any background. Bo thought it was the same reason she was so good at fighting, too; however, Sally stood her ground that the skills came from her self-defense courses. Whatever it took to keep her practicing was all Bo cared about right now. At the moment she had five contenders, minus Don with his lost limb, and was still holding her own. She used that same trick with the glowing light to create a lance, putting it in the ground to support her arching swing, and effectively knocking down her first opponent. Her foot lit on the ground for another push toward the next attacker. Sally swung back into the air, releasing the light pole to rocket her foot dead center of the next target, dispatching the last attacker with a burst of energy from her hands before rolling to a stop. Bo was stunned at the feeling of pride Sally stirred in him.

At first he thought it was the proud feeling he got when a student exceeded expectations but soon realized he had been around her for too long to be that naive. She was forcing him to face the past he tried hard to bury. If it wasn't for the last woman he had any relations with Bo might have tempted fate with Sally. The allure of that other woman and her betrayal of his trust kept him from wanting anything from another female again. Thinking of that wench made it easy to forget his feelings.

All her fighters were close to the same skill as him, so he could watch from the sidelines instructing Sally on mistakes she made. Yes, she hated him most of the time for doing just that, but she learned from it just the same. Wayward feeling pestered him to the point he feared they might get in the way when a real fighting started. The result would be using his judgment to protect her and possibly ending it for both of them.

Time always seemed short around Bo. A man able to live forever, yet always lived in the moment instead. Planning what to do next was one of those moments. They would leave soon to hide out somewhere safe until the Church forgot about her. Mexico was a good place to start; it had that Old World appeal he always craved. Almost reminding him of home.

The radio Sally had insisted on using during her workouts was just finishing a song when a news report –

rising in volume – broke in about a kidnapper or kidnappers lurking in the surrounding area of Colorado Springs taking women with reddish-brown hair, around five-and-a-half feet tall, and between ages of eighteen to thirty-five. Bo heard the reporter mention a few dead and others hurt but alive. The Cross was definitely on the hunt for Sally and seemed to have moved on to dirtier tactics in finding their prey. The description fit Sally too well for it not to be some random serial killer.

Bo couldn't help but take notice of the changes occurring around camp after word spread about Sally's skills. Her training had moved along nicely in both fighting and magic, but because of one exception, when accidentally took over one of the younger undead momentarily during a nerve-wracking practice fight; most of the camp's inhabitants began voicing their demands for Sally's removal. Lines were being drawn in the sand too often for them to stick around much longer anyway. Heading out this weekend suited him just fine with so many travelers on the roadways to mask their movements.

"Finish it up soon, Sally. We have to ready our plans or wing it from here. I am one that prefers a plan," Bo shouted out over the ruckus she and her combatants made.

He looked back to see her in a flying kick, again bringing out that red light rod to stab the ground after impacting the first fighter. Using leverage against it to spring the rest of the way up to her last opponent, she swiped the rod in a downward arch severing the upper half of his body from the lower section, letting loose entrails, then rolling to a stop. Sally walked back to her defeated attacker and helped him pull back together. She was getting less squeamish about blood and guts lying about the ground these days.

She is really good, Bo thought again, grinning with admiration and a touch of something more. *Enough of that, not the time or place for such matters in my life, let alone thoughts.*

The bigger question loomed over their head. Were they doing the right thing, teaching her skills that might one day bite back?

Moving off to one of the buildings Sally was given Bo entered the unlocked cabin and sat down to wait while pulling out a map he used to plan their route. When they made it to Mexico he would stick around a few months before leaving her to go back to the States, back to his secluded life. Bo had only been with her for a month, yet a bond was growing that he did not care for. He could remember the last time someone affected him in such a way. That woman wasn't human either, might never have been.

Interrupting his thoughts, Sally entered the small living space, enough to hold a bed and a meager table and chair, where Bo was sitting at the moment. When he motioned for her to sit she said, "What's up, boss?"

"We're moving up the game plan ourselves—that is, if you didn't pay any attention to the broadcast." Her blank stare revealed all he needed to know, "You should be paying more attention to what's going on around you and not just the guy in front of you. You might as well not even know how to fight for all that is doing you.

"The news report said killers are down south kidnapping women with your description, which means that The Cross is on to us and we need to scram."

"Oh, that. I heard it but didn't think about the connection. This is all still new to me; I mean getting hunted down and all. What's a girl to do?" Sally said sitting down on the bed with a thump, eyes turned up in asking.

Bo just laughed, "Don't try to play me like that. I've seen what you can do, and the defenseless act I won't buy."

"Fine."

"Fine."

Sally brought the conversation back around. "Do we still have a place to hide out in? Does this change anything else we might have already thought of? I'd still like to see some of the sights, too."

"Come to think of it, everything we've worked towards is a wash. Hence the reason I called you away from the training. We can still make it to Mexico with little issue, but a safe house is only safe when no one knows where it is. Somehow that doesn't seem to be the case anymore. Buying a place new might throw up flags we would rather see stay down, and our last option I can think of is staying with a trusted friend," Bo finished with more defeat in his voice than he wanted.

"What'd you mean about not buying a safe house? I get staying away from one already in place, but it should be safe, I would think, buying it with a fake ID." She looked at him truly baffled.

"A foreigner buying property, even with a fake US identification, is a bigger flag than I am willing to risk," he said plainly enough to douse further conversation.

They sat discussing the route and what they would need for the trip, both on the States side and in Mexico. A few stops along the way for some phone calls to arrange housing and another to get a car bearing Mexican plates for changing out with after crossing the border were on top of the list to do. Bo left her to clean up and headed back down to the shaman for any advice he might share.

But he doubted it. Larry kept tightlipped most of the time about pretty much everything. Wandering across the so-called courtyard took some time, and Bo reveled in it. Alone time was his favorite time of the day or night, or really any given time he found it. Bo reached the entrance relaxed from the peaceful walk and descended into the shaman's domain.

**

Sally said her good-byes to the few not giving her the cold shoulder because of her unwanted skills. She felt offended by the way the others were treating her. Shaking Don's hand fondly, she picked up her backpack to walk over where Bo was loading the car with their things. She had pared down the purchases made back in Colorado Springs, handing them out to some of the local women in the camp.

Bo had said it would only take about a week without sleeping to get where they needed to be. Her clothes would be fine until they crossed the border making her look more a tourist than a local. That would be fixed once they found the local dress shop to outfit her properly. A week's drive without sleeping meant they would end up deep into the country, if not the bottom of Mexico. She would have to remind him under no certain terms that they would have to stop for longer than a fill up. She didn't want to sleep too many times in the car.

He closed the trunk and circled the car, inspecting the tires before he got in the driver's seat. She hopped in and looked at Bo to ask, "Why haven't I driven us around yet?

I know you know where you're going, but I can follow directions if you give me a chance."

He looked back at her with a straight face. "You died in a car crash and I should just hand over the keys to you?"

CHAPTER 19

The ride back out of the mountain was uneventful, unlike the way up over a month ago. Sally's reaction to the magical barriers was not as dramatic as the first time because of the training Larry had given her, thankfully. Besides the dull headache left from passing through the barrier, all went smooth for once—no mysterious fog with werewolves lurking in wait or anything else.

They cut across the outskirts of Denver, Colorado, to hit I-25 south, which stretched all the way to Texas. It would not take long to find one of Mexico's numerous border crossings once they got close enough. Small talk passed the time between a stop for drinks and to fill up the gas tank. Finally Sally felt grumbling from her stomach and refused Bo's suggestion for a drive-thru, insisting instead on sitting somewhere other than the car before her imprint in the seat became permanent. Bo relented, proposing the stop be in Castle Rock, Colorado, to keep up their steady speed before it dropped below 75 mph inside town limits.

The Castle Rock Outlet Mall loomed ahead on the right. The exit ramp looped back around to the north as if circling the restaurant Bo had chosen, Smoke and Bones BBQ. This one might have been an inside joke for Bo the way he grinned as they parked. The parking lot for the restaurant was packed and they were forced to pull in near the ramp where space had been cleared for future development. It seemed pretty lively; people stood around waiting for tables to empty, and smells drifted out from the exhaust pipes on the roof floated down, enticing the surrounding shoppers to draw near and eat. Sally's stomach rumbled. The light breeze also carried a chill on it's underbelly, warning of the bitter cold winter still to come for the next few months.

Hopping out of the car, Sally felt rejuvenated at the prospect of getting knee deep in barbeque sauce. As they approach the front doors, they could hear music playing a mix of rock and alternative style music. This was going to be just what the doctor ordered as far as Sally was concerned. It seemed that Bo's nerves were getting raked over hot coals at hearing her choice of music so far. Rock was something he wanted to put into his ears, not listen to he'd told her. Sally decided she could take a nap after this meal and give him control over the knob. *Only fair*, she thought.

Feedback noise briefly rang out of the restaurant's speakers during the song "Actions and Motives" by 10 Years. She was getting familiar with the annoyance. The song got louder on the chorus line: "Bear the cross, wear the crown, just so evil you can't bleed out," which by the second chorus Sally grasped the meaning. It meant only one thing: The Cross must be in the vicinity. Her guardian angel that gave her a gift for premonition – or whatever it might be – called out to her in warning. Bo was oblivious to what had just transpired, and she gently grabbed his elbow to give him a push away from the restaurant.

Bo brushed it off, turning to her. "What're you up to now? I thought you were hungry—or did you change your mind?"

Looking back at him angrily, she said, "I was trying not to draw attention to us backpedaling to the car. I guess the premonition fairy didn't enlighten you to the presence of the Church as it did me. Now, can we hightail it out of here before I'm spotted?" She no longer felt safe out in the open parking lot and moved with a purpose to the car, sparing a glance now and again to see if there was anyone following them. Feeling they were in the clear, she reminded Bo to pull out as if they were everyday shoppers.

"You think I've never done this before? Been around slightly longer than you have fighting off the Church," he protested back.

"Sorry, just really nervous right now with all the cloak and dagger going on," Sally barked as she snapped the seat belt in place, blushing profusely.

Bo pulled out of the makeshift dirt parking lot up for sale, returning to the paved road. Habit had him constantly looking in the rearview mirror for a tail. He didn't notice any cars speed up when they hit the freeway and felt a little more relaxed as he eased into traffic. The sun was only a few hours from setting to help them run under the cover of darkness, which was how he preferred to move in on any given night. There was more power at their fingertips if need be.

They would be out of the woods when the Colorado boarder was behind them, at least that's what he hoped. A car zipped past them in the left lane, exceeding the speed limit. Bo to grab the steering wheel tightly for the eventual bump that would run them off the road, but it never came. He would pay more attention to the mirrors until the "Welcome to New Mexico" sign passed before relaxing any more. Miles passed without incident when the next off ramp exit approached and another car zigzagged through traffic, closing the distance between them.

Bo wondered if this car, too, was just another driver in a rush homeward bound. *Better to prepare for a nudge instead of playing it passively*, he warned himself.

"Hold on" was all he said to Sally. As the other car close the distance between them, the driver glanced repeatedly in their direction, giving off the telltale sign that he was not just a commuter trying to beat the evening traffic.

The other car veered to the right, hard, in an attempt to spin their car. Bo had been ready for that and turned the wheels to the left just as the pursuer hit them. Adjusting for the bump, Bo gunned the car and pulled back to the left, clearing the pursuer's car as the Church thugs reeled to the right and hit a guardrail. Oblivious drivers crashed into the Church's wrecked car. A few cars swerved to miss the building pileup, barely clearing the wreckage in time. Other cars, seeing what had happened, slowed to a stop.

Taking the opportunity the crash presented; Bo kept the pedal floored. He tried putting distance between them and the crash, but then he saw another car pull out from around the crash. "Has to be another Church vehicle on our tail again," he whispered angrily to himself. The chase was back on.

Bo swerved back and forth through the lightened traffic from people pulling over to watch the chaos unfold from the accident. What little distance he'd gained by his efforts fell apart when the shattering of the back window distracted him from his weaving through traffic.

"They can't kill us with bullets! What's the point of shooting at us? Too many people are on the road that might get hurt!" Sally exclaimed, outrage growing in her voice. She started to raise her hands, planning to retaliate.

"Hold up now. We don't expose ourselves by throwing magic around for others to see just because those idiots can't keep a secret." Steering around another car Bo replied, "Killing isn't their purpose, anyway; slowing us down is. Enough regular bullets drain the body of magic as it tries to repair our bodies. We won't be able to do much more."

"Didn't think of it that way," she said while watching the pursuer dart around a passing car, narrowly missing it to get closer.

"I think they're far enough back for us to lose them soon. Get ready for the next off ramp," he said changing lanes to the far left.

The Air Force Academy exit was coming up fast in the next mile, giving way to surface streets. That would give them enough advantage if Bo could use the street lights as leverage. What came up first was a forgotten element, road construction. Traffic gave them no choice except to get off the highway. They were expanding I-25 to three lanes, and people seemed to slow down gawking at the road crews and what they were working on. It was almost as bad as the drivers that had slowed to stare at the accident earlier. Bo had to cut back over fast or get pinned in.

Bo had to hit the emergency lane, a patch of road set aside for broken down cars, if he wanted to make the exit. Cars were already moving past the end of the exit with a green traffic light. He rounded the slowly curving three-lane exit, crossing back into traffic from the median to hit the middle left turn lane.

Dirt billowed from the emergency lane as the car behind them went wide, steadying out before going over the embankment. Bo hit the end of the lane as the street light turned yellow. He gunned it again to flash through the intersection, tires screeching around the turn, barreling down the overpass. Cars to either side saw him and followed his lead to beat the light, hampering the Church's closing gap with a cascade of vehicles.

Clearing the overpass, Bo brought the car closer to the speed limit; or enough to keep law enforcement off of them after he turned south onto N. Academy Boulevard past the Chapel Hills Mall. A few random left and right turns later had them pulled up behind a busy strip mall. He didn't feel yet that the coast was clear of any pursuit. Using the time wisely he pulled together his thoughts.

Bo turned to her finding Sally too shaken from the pursuit to speak either. There was just no other way to calm her down except with a reassuring voice and a little light contact to bring her back to now. Tingling raced across the palm of his hand when he put a hand on her arm, making him withdraw too quickly startling Sally out of her comatose. The magic in her reacted, too, putting the car's engine to a sputtering stop.

"Sorry," she said to the silence, staring down at her hands.

Probably the wrong time to tell her to stop being sorry for what she still can't control, he sadly thought.

He went the softer route instead, "It's OK. Just do the calming methods Larry taught you and things will be back to normal again," he paused long enough to see she was listening. "First car chase, I take it?" he asked, drawing out a nervous laugh from her.

She closed her eyes and slowed her breathing with an effort. He watched her control the magical spikes eddying through her very soul. A challenge after such an adrenaline high. The effort of calming herself nearly put her to sleep. Bo sat ready to hold her shoulder keeping Sally from falling over. Sally opened her eyes to see Bo staring at her before he averted his own. Settling back down in her seat, hunger began to beat down her need for sleep, her stomach rumbling in kind.

"We're going to change our plans. They know our location now," Bo said to the growing silence. "I think The Cross is being a bit more aggressive than they have been in the past. I haven't seen them want an undead as badly as they want you—never this bad in the past. We need to find refuge, and that means the South Camp with Mathyas."

"OK, who's Mathyas?"

"Mathyas is considered the leader for the western portion of the United States. He's the one that sent me to find you. I don't think it should be a problem, but news of what happened back in the northern camp may have made its way south already."

"Are we close enough to make it before The Cross spots us again? I would hate to go through that all over," she said. "Oh, and is there a drive-thru on the way? I'm not in the mood to have a sit-down meal anymore." Bo started laughing.

They pulled out from behind the strip mall slowly, watching for the car that chased them. Leaving the Briargate area, they meandered through side streets avoiding any main streets until reaching Uintah Street. Old Colorado City lay ahead with it's Victorian style houses and lazy streets. Business signs turned on facing the street as they made their way south through growing dusk.

A quick stop for burgers and fries satisfied Sally enough to go on. On the way to the Broadmoor, another subdivision of Colorado Springs, as they followed the signs to Helen Hunt Falls. Traversing the various side streets brought them to the narrow dirt road circling Bear Creek Park. Driving to the top of the access road, they looked down on Helen Hunt Falls with its man-made tunnels through the mountainside, giving them a view of the countryside.

On the downward leg of the road, Bo pointed out Upper Gold Camp Road, cutting its way along the upper reaches of the mountain. "The road was closed for repairs," he said. "However, this is just one more deterrent placed by the undead to ward off unwanted visitors."

CHAPTER 20

"Lost them?"

If Demric looked into a mirror he was sure he would see flames shooting out of his eyes. He could not believe his team had the girl in their sights and bungled the whole thing. *This isn't the kind of news I needed right now with those assholes breathing down my neck, waiting for this very kind of opportunity to castrate me.*

The detailed report from one of the lower ranking members explained why he gave the current updates instead of the captain Demric assigned. A crash on the freeway leaving Denver killed four of their men and injured two. The men he trusted most to run this operation stupidly piled up in one car to bring down the girl and ended up dead. Now all he had left were their underlings to do his bidding. *Could things get any worse?*

Knowing threats from afar would mean little to these men, he instead said, "She won't be far from where you last saw them. Call the other teams and position them south of that area quickly. I doubt they jumped back on the freeway so soon after being chased. There's still a good chance to corral them in Colorado Springs."

He could not fathom how he ended up hiring such utter fools. Demric heard panicked stuttering from the newly appointed officer starting up on the other end of the call, rage took over in his voice as he exclaimed, "No more excuses! Don't bother calling back until you have her."

Slamming the phone's receiver down to end the call, he stood up looking for something to destroy. He had been stressed out for days waiting on any phone call to come in with good news. Mike had not contacted him since the last time and now this mind-numbing report of such failure from his own men kept him in a bad mood. Murmuring from the closet in his office caught his attention.

Turning to the door with a renewed enthusiasm, he addressed the bodiless voices within, "I am *so* glad you decided to talk amongst yourselves. Had you been quiet I might have looked for some other outlet to take my aggression out on, but here you are to help me out. How about a nice game of soccer?"

CHAPTER 21

Dusk had settled into place by the time they hit the first tunnel on Upper Gold Camp Road. Night loomed in the distance with stars peeking through cotton white clouds from the twilit sky. Evening descended on the drive up, clouds dropped to cover mountaintops as they set to blanket everything else. "Are we always going to run into fog when we find these camps? I didn't care for the last time fog rolled in, but that wasn't a natural fog either," Sally confessed, getting a little spooked.

Bo puffed out his cheeks in an attempt to hide the laugh but failed miserably. "You've lived here long enough to know that this time of the year makes the clouds hang this low. And no, this is just a coincidence." At least he hoped it was.

Winding along, the cliff road opened up to a vibrant meadow of wildflowers mixed with flowers of columbine hidden under a tree's shadow. Ahead the road branched off; the right side led to a forestry gate Sally was becoming familiar with. The obvious destination was the gate with a faint glow of magical energies emanating from it. She could see the boundary wards even at this distance. The spectacle almost resembled the Great Wall of China judging by how far it stretched in either direction. Sally prepared herself for the wards, silently speaking a mantra over and over again as Bo pulled up to the gate.

Repeating words to herself had been a trick Larry taught her for moments like these. No magic was needed to make it work, just an empty mind and a calming attitude. She opened her eyes to Bo standing a couple of feet from the gate waving his arms. This time she did not see him with the key ring he'd used before. She heard buzzing the air like a honeybee nest stood nearby. As the gate slowly swung open, Bo dropped his hands, satisfied. Sally wondered if he neglected using the key to save time or if it was showing off. By the time he got back in the car the gate stood wide open.

"They use magic a bit differently here with convenience being more important than actual labor," Bo explained. "It means more time taken to maintain the spells in working order but less time getting their hands dirty."

Sally looked back to see the gate slowly closing up.

Bo continued, "This is going to be a culture shock to you compared to the North Camp's daily routine. Try not to look too surprised with what you see. Larry left this place because the demand on him was too much, leaving him little time to do things for himself. What you should know is…"

Bo began to say. A boulder flew out of the rolling fog, arching for the car's path. He had no time to veer away, and the rock smashed the hood, stopping the engine dead. Steam gushed from under the demolished hood.

Not far from the gate they'd entered, short greenish colored forms emerged from the trailing edges of the fog from all directions almost completely encircling the car.

The creatures' ears had more hair gathered in tufts near the points than the tops of their heads, and sharply pointed teeth protruded through sickening smiles. They stopped short of the vehicle as taller forms walked out of the fog dressed in some Victorian style garb, four of them in total. Elegant wasn't even close to how these people presented themselves as they strode to the front of the car. Getting a closer look with the help of the headlights, Sally saw their eyes were pitch black, skin a pasty white under the gloom of the enveloping darkness.

"Great. I thought we could make it to the camp before true night set in. Before this scum woke up to be a problem." Bo forced the words through gritted teeth.

Sally looked at the surrounding group gathered outside the car once more, "I can tell these aren't werewolves like the last time. These people have an alluring appeal to them that I can't quite shake."

"That's because they're vampires. Those other things are ghouls they use as henchmen. Human servants are only good for a few things, such as food and going into town during the day for any errands," Bocnic said under his breath.

"Then what's their problem?"

Bo considered the answer before laying it out for her. "They have a grudge with the truly undead. We walk in daylight, they can't. We will live forever; they can die under the right circumstances. Just to name some highlights.

"They want what we have and are continually picking fights in the hopes of find a way to kill us permanently."

Bo's door opened of its own accord as tendrils of fog reach in to coax him out. "Please join us if you would," one of the vampires said, "so we might talk civilly."

There was just too much venom underlining those words for Sally to believe him. Her door opened in the same manner as Bo's to invite her out into the night. The vampires stood perfectly still as they waited. One of the other vampires with blond hair spoke up as if reading her mind: "We won't wait all night for your company. Don't make us come to you and help you out of your seats."

"Let's get it over with. You should know they are very fast on their feet, so don't let go of one if they attack," Bo said with a wink. "No need to whisper either, they can hear most everything we say," And with that he unbuckled his seat belt exiting the car.

"Now that's better, isn't it?" the blond vampire said. "I almost thought you had lost your manners, Bocnic. So sorry about your car getting crushed, too. Our little helpers sometimes don't care for other people's property like they should, and from the way the conversation in the car went I take it the girl is a new addition."

"Where are your manners, Bo? Are you not going to introduce us to your lovely lady friend? We do like to make new acquaintances," the first vampire said.

"Always the pompous one aren't you, Victor." Bo spat the words at the closest one with dirty blond hair. "Sally, meet Victor here in his entire splendor, Brogden with the red hair and flamboyant flair for clothes to match, and Warren—but I haven't met your companion. I assume he is just as new," Bo finished with ire rising in his voice.

"His name is—" Victor was interrupted and the irritation of being interrupted showed.

"My name's Dr. Jack because I have a PhD in jacking you up! Show me a—"

Near shouting from Victor brought Dr. Jack to heel. The smack across the back of the head followed through on the point. "Silence! We will teach you how and when to speak in public later." Victor steamed at the impertinence of his underling's outburst. "My most sincere apologies," he said to Bo and Sally, dripping sincerity. "Now where were we? Oh yes, introductions. We hail from the Dul'Clome family that resides in these parts." He bowed to the waist, never taking his eyes off Sally.

Glancing over at Bo to find the right words, she took a chance. "Would I say this is a pleasure? If so, I am honored." She surmised this might be the correct response from Bo's expression.

"Are we done with the pleasantries?" Bo seemed to be tiring of the vampires quickly.

In the blink of the eye they were no longer out in front. Victor stood behind Bo, gripping his neck in one hand and using the other to twist his left arm behind his back. Brogden restrained Sally the same way. "Now we see what you're made of," Dr. Jack said from somewhere behind Sally's vision.

"Yes, I am quite done with formality," Victor whispered in Bo's ear as he used his other hand to twisted Bo's right arm harder behind his back, forcing a grunt of effort out of Sally's companion. Victor spoke up for the rest to hear him, "You two watch how this is done. There won't be a need for interfering as Brogden and I will make this quite entertaining for you."

Sally stood paralyzed not knowing what to do next. Training hadn't included vampires and was too new for a real fight. The only thing left that suggested any hope right now was her voice to summon magic, but as the first syllables crossed her lips, Brogden clamped down tight on her windpipe forcing silence. It might not be a problem for Bo, but she still needed air to live. She began feeling lightheaded and strained to think of something to remove the steel grasp from her throat. Sally kicked back with her leg to sweep Brogden's legs out from under him.

Nothing.

Not a damn thing, she thought.

Brogden belted out a deep, billowing laugh as he placed the foot she'd missed farther back on the ground. It was what she hoped for. Without telegraphing her movements this time, she swept out with the other leg, connecting a solid smack to the closer ankle. In the same motion, not wasting precious seconds, she bent at the waist, cartwheeling him over her shoulder. A kneejerk reaction made him release her to keep from marring his face as he went headfirst into the ground. Sally rolled the opposite way getting clear.

Still in her tumble, she rapidly croaked a few words, bringing the familiar reddish glow of her light rod to life. Planting the end in the dirt, she catapulted back landing on Brogden's shoulders before he could stand. Bo was right about slowing the vampire's momentum down with touch, but it didn't stop him; Brogden dragged her foot under him, and sank his sharp teeth into the calf near the ankle. He was rewarded with a high-pitched scream. A bond grew between them as he drank deeply of her blood, magic from both creatures mingling together.

You don't take advantage of a lady without at least asking first, Sally thought, letting her leg slip some more towards his head.

She thought the rod down to the manageable size such as a short sword since the magic allowed her to manipulate it easily once it was called upon. Her concentration began to waiver as blood seeped down

Sally's leg that was not sucked up by the vampire. She had to act soon. Waiting until the back of Brogden's head was visible, she swung with all her might while the preoccupied vampire sopped up her lifeblood.

Sizzling flesh burned when her rod cut across his scalp, revealing withered brain tissue beneath. Screaming ferociously, he released her leg and she broke free. She had wanted to aim for the neck to take off the head completely, but her own leg had been in the way, and Sally didn't want to take the chance of deforming herself in the midst of battle. Brogden stayed flat on his belly, not uttering another word.

"She's been taught well," Victor whispered into Bo's ear. "Too bad I will kill her after I kill you."

Bo grunted again as he brought the twisted arm back down to his side, "You haven't killed me yet with all the tries you've had so far. What makes you think I'm going to be any easier this time?"

He was still watching Sally from the corner of his eye as she got up off her knees, looking satisfied. Bo tried to yell out as Victor crushed his windpipe. Without his warning, Sally got the rest of the way up to take a fighting stance toward Victor. He just grinned back as she put her toughest warrior face on to intimidate her enemy.

She looked Bo's way as he flicked his eyes away fast then back to her. He repeatedly sent the message to her as a warning, she hoped, when he looked down. Taking a chance she went down, too—just in time, as Brogden picked up his missing top and used the sharpened bone's edge as a blade to fling at her. It missed her as she ducked, and Bo leaned forward at the last minute to put Victor in its path, catching his shoulder and severing it cleanly from the body.

Victor let loose of Bo, grabbing the wound with an angry screech. Brogden stood still, shocked at hitting Victor, just before he lunged lightning fast for Sally gripping a handful of her hair and forcing a quick scream of pain from her. A flash of light covered the ground in an iridescent glow and the surrounding air crackled as if on fire with electricity. Sally's magic took over in a millisecond of unconscious action.

Minutes passed before anyone could see again. What Bo saw stopped him in his tracks. The vampires stood stiff as statues, not a single movement seen from them. Just because he could, Bo took a swing at Dr. Jack's face, knocking his head back as precious blood began to drain from his nose.

"Bo," Sally warned, "this isn't the time to take out your aggressions on him for what he said."

Grabbing a limb from a nearby tree for an impromptu stake, Bo paused even if he knew the right action to take was stabbing these blood-suckers right there and then. He reluctantly stepped away saying, "All right, I'll back off, but we should kill them where they stand."

Sally ordered Victor and Brogden to retrieve their missing parts testing how far her powers went. They moved, even if the reaction was slow to follow. She said to Bo, "I am not so familiar with killing on a whim as you seem to be. I'd rather send them back from where they came from before putting mass slaughter on my resume."

Catching her breath from the fighting, she looked over in Victor's direction saying snidely, "I guess I was thoroughly entertained."

Bo sighed and shook his head. "Vampires only want one thing from us, and that is our immortality. Doesn't matter how many times we tell them it isn't something we can give. They just continue to kill us until we stay dead."

"Well, if that's how they want it to be…" Sally started to say as she watched Victor for a response. His eyes darted back and forth between them, showing he had more control of his body than his companions.

Sally finished by saying, "I will make an act of kindness this once and let them go back with the stipulation that they can never feed again."

Her control over the vampires was apparently weakening; Victor's eyebrows rose slightly at the statement, giving Sally a reason to smile. She did what she said, sending them on their way with stern orders to never eat again and watched them walk off into the distance. The ghouls just stood in a semicircle for a little longer before following their leaders. It appeared that they required orders to follow if they were going to do something, and none of the vampires ordered them at all. *Useless if you ask me*, Sally thought in disgust.

Bo looked back at Sally with slight concern, drawing his eyebrows together before inspecting the damaged car. Steam rose from the dented hood. The car had given up on them. Bo showed her the direction they were headed from here, to Sally's disappointment. That disappointment did not come from walking but from other possible run-ins they might have. She was not willing to go through that again for some time. Training for a fight was one thing; actually using those skills was very different. Knowing the opponent would kill you and might not stop there brought a shiver not conceived by the frigid winds stirring up. She resigned herself to walking the rest of the way, asking how much farther they would need to go. Bo told her it would be well past midnight at their current pace before they made it to the outskirts of the camp.

"Superb, an all-nighter with god knows what possibly lurking in wait for prey like us to stroll by," she snidely commented.

"Blah, blah, blah. Quit your whining and keep up," Bo snapped back.

Sounds like he might be just a little pissed from all the bad luck so far, Sally reflected. *Reaching the southern camp might cheer him up. OK, in a better mood would be just as good.*

CHAPTER 22

"How long before the vampires stop following your orders?" Bo questioned Sally. She was actually concerned over it, too. "What're the chances it wears off before we get close enough to camp to stop worrying?"

How much had Larry told him? She shook her head at his questioning, not knowing how to say it. "I don't have a clue. It wasn't something Larry wanted me to test, especially in his presence." Sally speculated, "You seemed to fare well. What is it now, three times I've done it, and not once have you been affected. Anyway, Victor showed signs of breaking the spell faster than the others. He showed independent movement; that's why I worked so fast to get them moving."

They had been walking some time for the position of the moon to be so high. It was almost overhead in the clearing sky. It seemed like days had passed at the rate they were walking, and Sally longed for a rest—if not full-on sleep then just a small catnap. Focusing on her time in the northern camp, she recalled Larry saying that one of these stars was the sign of her rebirth, but she couldn't remember which one now.

Still staring up at the sky counting stars, she took the chance to recall earlier events before continuing, "The next time Victor meets up with me there won't be another takeover for him. He might be old enough to hold it off." Temptation for power lingered in the back of her mind. "Unless I get stronger he will be a problem I'm not ready to face anytime soon. Don't look at me like that. Growing my power to control anything dead isn't something I'm working towards to defeat him either."

Relief passed over Bo's face so fast she might have imagined it. "Well, we'll pick up speed for a while to save time. Leaving them alive wasn't a good idea in the first place. We'll be watching our back the rest of the way so putting a larger gap between us and them isn't a bad idea either, just in case."

It seemed to her that Bo would honor her decision and leave the vampires alone despite his protests to do otherwise. She guessed he might not do the same the next time. Bo started looking back the way they had come, worrying Sally. He motioned to slow down to a walk. He didn't turn his head all the way as he had earlier; he just cocked it enough to listen for movement in the rear. She caught on fairly quickly as they progressed until she, too, heard the rustling of brush in the distance.

Bo motioned them to stop. He turned in the direction of the noise, standing his ground as the sounds grew closer. "Come out so we can see you," Bo said into the night. "We'll stand our ground until you do."

A deep voice rang out. "I didn't mean to scare you, Bocnic. We don't talk with many nowadays." The crunching of leaves and branches echoed out of the darkness as it grew even closer.

Sally exclaimed, "Werewolf!" before bring her glowing light rod to hand.

The faint light gave off enough to show a figure with hair head to toe. "Forgive us, Ancient One," Bo said, bowing deeply. "We didn't know you were in the wood with us."

Sally forgot her fighting stance in wonderment at Bo's reaction to this intruder. The Ancient One looked familiar to her somehow, but not in the werewolf sort of way she'd first thought. He stood over six feet tall, with scraggly brown hair covering his body and an apish form to his face. He reminded her of a show on TV, but that didn't make sense. Still, she couldn't shake the feeling of seeing this creature somewhere.

Coming out of her thoughts, she listened to Bo continue, "What can we do for you?"

Silence stretched as the creature's eyes burned into her, measuring her worth more than what she looked like. "I came to congratulate your apprentice in her skills fending off your attackers, but moreover, her choice when dealing with them."

He spoke this time in her direction. "Dear lady of the walkers, I overheard your name to be Sally. I am called Adelwin, and I am honored to meet you," he said, tilting his head in a manner of a bow.

"I guess I'm just as honored," she replied, bemused.

"No need to fake respect with me. You evidently have not been given all the knowledge this one possesses"—Bo seemed to blush at the statement as much as she could tell from her glowing rod—"and you can drop the rod. I will not attack. Let me provide proper lighting so we may continue."

As her own light faded, it was replaced by a ball of iridescent blue light the size of a softball. Adelwin found a fallen tree to sit on, and as he settled in he never took his eyes off of her. "What questions do you have, young one?"

Sally was caught off guard by the question and stuttered, "What are you?"

"That, my friend, is a long story for another time. Let us use a term you might know better: Bigfoot."

Shock took her at the memory of watching *In Search Of* with her parents as a child.

"Not too many believers out there hunting us down for a photo-op these days," Adelwin said with some humor. "Yes, I said *us*. We were the first to change before man outgrew the trees. Over many years some of us have moved on, but we still try to guide the younger of our kind on the right paths." Sorrow filled his eyes as he spoke of the loss. "I'll give you a better time line. I was born in the age of dinosaurs. Scientists dubbed us Neanderthals. You might even call us the missing link."

Bo stared, mystified at hearing undead actually died or was *moving on* a relative term used for leaving. He was too shaken to bring up the question as Adelwin continued, "Time is short, as the vampires won't stop walking home until your magic fades, which isn't much longer. We do not have the time to finish the historical lesson, but I would like to spend more time with you and maybe sharpen some of those skills you have. The threat you have been made to think you are is not completely true. I see in you the potential others that carried the gift never cared to think of; only power enveloped their lives.

You showed compassion to those that wanted to kill you; it took more to walk away than fall to their level. I commend you. When you return to these mountains, search me out and I will find you. We have so much to teach you, which no other can. We alone hold those secrets close to our heart."

Adelwin stuck out his hand, and Sally reached out apprehensively. Skin touched skin, causing the air to vibrate with a hum of force while a light display beyond words flared to life. The deepest of night vanished from the strobe of light centered between their palms. Sally exhaled to find no air coming back into her lungs. Panic spread from her head to her limbs in a shaking mess. Adelwin released his grip, and the world spun in a dizzying circle. She was sure the world was revolving around her at the speed things were moving across her vision. Once everything came to a stop, she followed the brightness back to the Ancient One for guidance about what just happened. A headache began to form from the experience, not a ride she wanted to take again.

"That bit of magic will let me know when you enter the wood again. Farewell, and good luck getting to your destination," Adelwin said with his back to them. "I will fend off any pursuers that might follow."

"Thank you for your kindness, Great One," Bo called. "May you travel with good tidings."

"And to the both of you."

After Adelwin had moved out of sight did they strike out in their own direction. Sally looked over to Bo. "Does the day get any stranger? I don't know if I can take much more," she exclaimed in a near hysterical tone.

"Can't say that I blame you. We're good, except for the yearly paranormal get-togethers." That drew a paranoid look from her. "I'm kidding. Calm down, I can see I should learn when a joke is appropriate. The answer is no, even *we* don't run into each other this often."

"Undead, the Church chasing us, werewolves and vampires trying to kill us, and back to the undead seems to be a bit much. My dance card was filled before we even left the north camp!" Sally nervously laughed that out, barely.

A few miles of trotting brought them close to the south camp. The moon had passed its zenith during their talk with Adelwin, and morning wasn't too far off, keeping the vampires at bay unless they were looking for a very deep tan. From the high point Bo had brought her to, she could see movement below marking the camp's interior. Another set of wards encircled the camp with its own brilliant light, making the torches seem useless. At a walk they would make it in an hour tops, which was what they intended to do to cool off from the fast pace they'd been keeping. They talked openly not for the conversation but to warn any sentries of their presence. It worked so well that they had more than a handful of guards surrounding them.

The guards asked them to stand fast while a representative was brought. Bo thought it odd, but security measures might have been raised with the Church in town. There was small chatter between the guards and even less to the temporary captives searching for shelter.

CHAPTER 23

A small entourage could be seen making its way in the waning moonlight to Bo and Sally's location. Bo hoped to speak to Mathyas soon about the latest events. His hope soon came to fruition as Mathyas himself join the party outside the camp. He walked up close to the two of them with a quick greeting, though his eyes never left Sally.

"Whom have you brought to our modest camp, Bocnic? She is a lovely piece of work." While Mathyas spoke his pleasantries, Bo watched as a few of his entourage continued to walk the outskirts of the meeting, finally standing behind them.

"This is Sally Mertill." Bo gestured in her direction. "I have been tutoring her in our ways, but you already knew that part. You're the one that sent me to find her." He tried to get a feel for where Mathyas was going.

"Please, let me be the first of the southern clan to welcome you to our humble dwellings," Mathyas said, the words well rehearsed since he used them every time someone new entered the camp. He bowed at the waist to show his respect and expected the same back.

Bo nodded to Sally to follow his lead and returned the greeting. Recovering from his own bow, movement from behind caught his attention too late. Hands reached out for the both of them as Bo turned to meet the charge full on, getting knocked to the dirt floor. Sally wheeled on her heels, but her attacker carried a club and took her on the side of the head, knocking her down. Bo grappled with the guard as they rolled away from the center of the malformed circle and from Sally. With horror he saw why he was rolled away. Golden cuffs were being clasped on Sally's wrists.

A whirlwind of events unfolded as the last clasp locked into place. Wind blew loose dirt and debris in all directions, slowly forming an unstable dirt devil. The bits of dirt and rock in the windstorm pelted the surrounding people. Sally lay in the middle of it all, head lolling back and forth like she wanted to shake away the demons tormenting her in her own head. A deep purple light erupted from the center of her chest and expanded, losing intensity the farther away it got from her. The closest people to the intense light caught fire, dropping to the ground to roll themselves out.

As fast as it had started, everything stopped with such suddenness it was hard to believe anything ever happened. Sally still lay on her side, but now her right side burned its own orange fire from within. Most had squatted to the ground avoiding what they could of the action, keeping on their feet if there was a need to bolt. Mathyas stood through the whole thing without blinking an eye, using his magic to keep him safe. Numerous shields popped out of existence after Sally's fanfare died off. A pompous smile sat on his face, making Bo wanted to take him then and there, but he knew better to attack the head of this faction.

"Pick her up and take her to the camp. She must have had a protective spell woven to cause such a ruckus, however short-lived." Mathyas waved a hand, expecting his followers to do his bidding. The orange glow rapidly diminished and finally faded before he could utter the last of his sentence.

"Why did you attack us? We came looking for shelter for Christ's sake!" Bo stood, enraged at the way she was being treated. "Council will hear me out before the day starts."

"Why would they care what the likes of you has to say? Stay or be gone, I care not what you do from here." With that Mathyas turned returning to camp without even a single look back.

Sally was pushed unceremoniously forward toward the camp with Bo on her tail while the clan members followed. Hushed words rapidly being passed between the group led to one thing, Sally's magical outburst. He had to admit that what she'd done back there was not something he had seen before, and he doubted Mathyas had either. Bo looked around at the woods they walked through picking up a dizzying affect made by a discreetly manipulated spell to ward off people in the surrounding area, making a traveler lose his or her sense of direction.

"What's up with the extra security measures since I was last here?"

"Surely you got word the pesky Church is snooping around these parts and our location is to be hidden at all costs from them," Mathyas retorted briskly.

"Yeah, we bumped into them a little while ago"—Bo felt Mathyas's eyes burn the back of his neck—"and we lost them around the north end of town, so they didn't follow us here."

"Good for you," Mathyas said back with venomous zeal, "or we might've had to imprison you, too."

"Your threats ring hollow to me. Unless I actually do something to break our laws, keep them to yourself."

Mathyas's quick intake of breath told Bo enough. There would not be any retaliation of their word play yet. Mathyas had time to find something else to take Bo down with later. They trudged the rest of the way in silence, Sally walking unaware of her surroundings given what she'd just endured. Concern for her mental state bothered Bo more than anything physical she could have suffered. She'd told him during her weeks of training how the memories of other handcuffed people ran through her when the gold touched her skin. What she got from the memories still wasn't clear to him, but the show of strength he just witnessed might have been her way of using that knowledge to retaliation.

The layout of the camp matched most other camps around the country with few exceptions. The reason for coordinating the camps to be similar was to keep visiting members from getting too lost while in a camp. One exception some camps had was a working jail to hold prisoners for judgment. Each major camp, like any state capital, had a jail, a closed council hall, and other minor changes to make a camp stand out from the other. The added parts also were never in the same spot as another camp to keep invaders from attacking and in this case jail breaking of any prisoners.

There was a bustling in the camp as they all entered the outer reaches. Sally was ushered off to the cages at the back of the camp while the rest followed Mathyas out to parts unknown. Bo looked for familiar faces and branched off from the group to search out those people he could trust.

He waded through the throng of people milling about after the display of Sally's capture, making it slightly more difficult to find a friendly face or two. Few acknowledged Bo's presences with a fast hello or good day as he wound his way through the crowd. Morning broke before he found anyone to talk with. Time was growing short before Mathyas did something rash. He was sure to do something by nightfall, if he was not already gathering followers at this very moment.

Before Bo could find Michal, the witch Zemra drew his attention. She stood not far off from one of the out buildings hidden under a tree. There was always something for her to talk about. She couldn't resist using her ability to say a thing or two about everything under the sun. There was a good chance she might let something slip because of her over bearing pride in the skills of foretelling. Michal could wait if Zemra could be persuaded.

He made a beeline to where she stood as Zemra looked his way with a knowing smile, and his heart sank as she threw up a hand to ward off anything Bo might have said. "Is there any need to bother me about the girl? Her fate is sealed," she exclaimed righteously.

"What fate?"

"It was written in the stars before she was reborn that the Slaver would return." Zemra's otherworldly voice echoed out of the wrinkled sack she wore for a face.

"More hindsight than foretelling if it's true, unless you meant to keep the information quiet while Mathyas sent me to collect Sally," he retorted, playing dumb but realizing too late his mistake—never cross a witch.

"Some things must come to pass if they are to be corrected. Stopping what was to come would only create the chance for another to be reborn. The fact that she lives blanks out from my mind what could've been."

"You still haven't told me her fate. It seems clear enough that she is going to be executed with not much of a trial." A nod of her head was all he got. "I'm going to do what I can to prevent that."

The witch's beady eyes bored through him. "Trial is set for tonight. Not much time to prepare anything to save your precious girl." Zemra spoke through a grin cracking her face with the stench of smugness.

Feeling he was wasting his time now, Bo said his farewells and moved on to find Michal, hoping there was more to glean from him.

CHAPTER 24

Sally gradually regained control of her footing as she was guided to an area of shimmering bars—or that was what they looked like with her vision still blurry. Guards stood at the ready to open the barred door to her cell, and a quick struggle proved only that the guards had a firm grip on her arms and they were not going to let go. There was no opportunity for escape with these burly men holding on. She hoped one would open up later.

The guards tossed her in the cage without so much as a word. Sally tucked into a ball using some of the momentum and the skills she'd learned to spring back at the entrance as the barred door closed. But the guards were quicker than she was, and locks fell in place before she could reach the cell door. With the door closed, she felt the rest of her energy leaving her completely empty. The other times she'd interacted with the gold riveted her with a backlash of force when the nauseating metal touched skin. Sally felt new members added to the growing collection of people floating incoherently across her memories. *Getting knocked out before the handcuffs got put on would do it*, she thought.

She had little else to do except inspect her new surroundings. The bars encompassed everywhere she looked. Sally could even feel them reaching for her underfoot. It made sense to keep prisoners from digging their way out. Human guards stood outside the cell watching her pace back and forth.

She didn't know what ran around her head half the time nowadays with experiences not her own to filter out. It was hard to think of anything with dislodged memories floating aimlessly through her mind. Too bad those recollections didn't give advice on escaping from gold.

How many humans worked for the undead gave her something else to think about. Was it the same reasons vampires used them, minus the need to have a person around for a light snack? It was obvious human guards were useful around gold and maybe purchasing things that required legitimate identification. Sure, there must be fanatics with every kind of supernatural species, but what were these people looking to get out working for the undead. Immortality?

Sally thought there would be no harm in striking up conversation with the guards. "What would it take to get something to drink around here?"

"We don't serve to captives," the one on the left snarled out. "Anyway, we won't fall for tricks like that from the undead. We know better; can't be a guard if you don't know anything about your kind otherwise."

"I'm not that old to not need a drink. Fine, have it your way," Sally said with a shrug. Trying another tactic, she asked, "What's going on here that puts me in a cage? We came for shelter."

"You're too powerful, as Mathyas puts it, to be let loose around the camp. No one wants to be under your power. We don't take kindly to having our little hidey hole disturbed," the guard on the right said with disdain.

"That's absurd! Why would I care to take over someone's camp?" Sally felt her blood rise. "I just wanted to stay clear of the Church's people until I could get to a safe place."

Nervousness crossed both of their faces at the mention of the Church, "Church is in the Springs?" one asked, speaking more to the other guard than to her.

"They cleared this area already. Should have been safe after they left," the other guard replied back, glaring to Sally.

So, they were not told what she was really capable of. Trust in the humans seemed to only go so far when it came to some secrets of the undead. The Church was also a surprise to them. No telling how much they knew or what she could say without letting anything out of the bag. No reason to give Mathyas anything else to nail her with since she already was locked down for being a Slaver. What was Mathyas going to do with her locked up anyway? Maybe Bo would have answers when and if he was allowed to visit her. God, she hoped he could visit just so she could see a kind face.

CHAPTER 25

Bo moved among the crowd as he went in search of Michal for information about what Mathyas knew. The afternoon sun was high above their heads before he spotted the man. His back was to Bo as he approached and tapped him on the shoulder. Michal jumped, turning quickly. Maybe the upcoming trial had him on edge.

Surprise still lit Bo's face as he greeted his friend. "How you been? Seem a little out of sorts today, eh?"

Michal's words came out rushed. "I guess after that flash up the hill where you were found and the fact we have a Slaver back in our midst might put anyone on edge. Of course the last Slaver was before my time so what I know is second hand. Her power is enough to frighten me."

Bo found nothing good to say at the moment that would sate his fears.

"Who wouldn't be shaken up?" Michal's eyes darted back and forth as if looking for someone to jump out any minute. "Of course if there as close to her as you are, what's to fear?"

Bo shrugged. "I suppose all the recent action must have most people jumping. All right, bad question. What's been going on around camp before we showed up then? Things have changed around here since I left. Feeling a little out of the loop." Bo thought that sounded more like an understatement than he wished.

"Can't talk about it. Orders from up high about anything surrounding the Slaver. That includes from the time of her birth." Looking ashamed Michal stared at the ground as he continued, "Sorry I can't do much more for you. Eyes and ears are everywhere, waiting for someone to slip up."

Bo saw an opening to get a small bit of revenge. "Zemra must feel she's above the law if she can speak about some of this to me."

Shock gave way to bemusement as Michal listened to Bo speak, "So she did, did she? Wonder what the future tells her about what Mathyas will think. Thanks."

With Zemra's slip out in the open, Bo took advantage of his friendship trying for more information. "You're welcome. Anything about the trial you might be willing to let slip? She already told me bad things were coming."

"Well, the only worry she should have is how they are going to handle her execution," Michal said with a shake of his head. "Time's wasting and I still have a few things that I have to attend to. We'll talk later, yes?"

A quick nod was all it took. Michal ran off fishing out a cell phone from his pocket as he went. Bo could not help but wonder where he was off to in such a hurry.

The coming trial looked bleak. There were only so many ways they could dismember a body, unless

Mathyas was busy dreaming up new and crueler ways to deal the sentence out. Bo would not put it past him to try out some new twisted torture to liven up the crowd. He had found out enough to head back to Sally and check up on her condition. She had to be scared. Maybe he could bring her fears to shallower waters.

CHAPTER 26

Sally had been pacing for hours trying to think of a way to get those guards away, but they were steadfast for humans, without so much as a need for drink or bathroom break. Requests for a chair, food, drink, or a trip to the bathroom were all denied. They told her everything she needed was already in there. Sally continued to pace the empty cage in an attempt to stave off a desire for sleep that had plagued her since entering these confines. If they had stopped during the trek to the camp, sleep would not be an issue right now. Gold was just becoming too much of a nuisance; no telling how long she would sleep if it took her now. The only thing Sally could think of was keeping quiet until the trial because the alternative was giving the guards reasons to misuse their power.

The thought was fleeting as Bo came striding down the dirt path to her. Sally's hopes rose as he got closer to the guards and they waved him on. His face gave away nothing until he noticed her looking. Then he put on a halfhearted smile—for her sanity, she assumed. This let on to things not going as well as he hoped. It did lift her spirits some in any case.

Bo reached her cell not saying anything until he looked back to check that the guards were out of earshot. Without touching the bars, he took her hand in his to comfort her. She felt a quick renewal of power when they joined hands, but that faded when he released hers.

"How you holding up?" Bo questioned, seeing the shadows under her eyes. He refused to show any weakness from the withdrawal he felt.

"Not good," she said with undertones of contempt. "I don't know how much longer I can hold out before taking a catnap. What's going on out there anyway?"

"Well, the good news is they are waiting for sunset to start, and that isn't much farther away. I'm working on defending you so you get out in one piece." He tried not to look away when he whispered more than spoke, "Odds of us winning aren't that good, but there is a chance we can sway them. Working the details out still, so bear with me."

She tilted her head to one side questioningly. "Haven't I already trusted you enough thus far for you to think I might just stop on a dime?" She smiled. "You haven't let me down yet. There is always a 'bad' following the 'good' news. Lay out the bad news already."

"Isn't it all bad news? This is how I think it will go tonight if the rules are followed. Like any other courtroom there will be a judge, prosecutor, and defender. Your jury will consist of the tribunal members in residence. Most often they make time for other camps to join in the decision making, but you are a special case." Bo checked again that the guards were out of earshot. "I sent a message to Larry for his help even though he isn't liked around here. He still holds weight with the tribunal over anything pertaining to magic. Let's hope he makes it."

"While we're waiting, could I get you to bring back something to eat or drink? Those asses think I've been around as long as you and won't so much as budge from their post." She felt as exhausted and she must look it. "It should keep me going until they walk me to the hearing."

Bo nodded, concern etched on his face. "I'll see what they have."

"Thanks."

As he was about to say something else, some of the locals came up to see Sally. They stared at her like she was an animal at the zoo caged for their protection. Maybe they were right to be cautious. She knew she'd always felt that way with the lion behind the bars. The stares started to get to her the longer they stood not saying a word, forcing her to be the first to look away.

Bo took it as his cue to get her things. He walked away, arms spread in an attempt to corral the spectators, telling them, "You'll see enough at the trial. No need to stand around gawking now."

Sally was not so sure she liked the way he said that. He would have to explain himself when he got back. Was that something he was about to tell her? She would just have to bide her time until Bo got back to find out.

CHAPTER 27

Night had fallen only moments before Sally saw the lit torches heading her way. It made her feel like she was in some B-rated movie when the villagers were gathering to take down the monster—expect this was reality, and she was the monster. Fear crept up from the pit of her stomach trying to expel what she had earlier from Bo. *Can't give them the satisfaction*, she thought.

The guards came to the cage door telling her to move back so they could open it without any funny business. Without much choice, she did as they told her and they escorted her out. It had only been a day in that cage but being released, even in handcuffs, still felt good. Sally looked to the darkened sky and felt an urge to stretch but held back in case the guards took it the wrong way.

She didn't see the stone coming until it was too late to ward off. She was struck, while staring up at the stars, under the chin near her throat. A sharp gasp escaped her as she looked back at the crowd, scanning the group for the perpetrator. Snickering from the guards made her mad as they pushed her forward. This time she saw the next rock coming and dodged to the left feeling it skim passed her cheek before the rock found a resting place in one guard's forehead.

"That's enough!" yelled the guard in front of her as he went around to check on his partner. Blood trickled down along the guard's brow from the gash the rock had left.

"One of you come here and carry Chuck to the doctor. The rest of you back off. Now I'm a man down because of your actions!" he said, berating the group. "The rest can just walk ahead of the prisoner while I watch the rear. We don't need any more violence; that'll come later." With that said, he winked at Sally causing a shiver that raced down her spine.

She was sure Bo had been going to tell her about the trial but never got the chance to say more than he had. When he had brought her the food and drink, the vigilant guards took it from him to inspect, then sent him on his way. There hadn't been another chance since then for them to talk. Something about tribunal law. She was on her own until this moving entourage got her to the trial area in one piece. At least she hoped the one guard left could keep it that way.

It wasn't far to walk from the cage to the center of camp. Her fear of the mob abated when the space cleared for the trial loomed ahead, surrounded by a semicircle of torches. Empty tables were set behind the torches with a podium stand set halfway and forward of those tables. *That must be where the judge will stand to give judgment*, Sally thought. Already another crowd separate from her escort had begun forming around the unlit areas of her makeshift trial, closing the circle without much effort.

To the far side of the formed circle, outside the range of torchlight, stood Bo. She could tell from his silhouette. When he saw her notice him, he made a gesture to his chin. She had almost forgotten what had happened earlier and reached a cuffed hand to her own chin, bringing a twinge of pain from the touch. She looked down at her hand to find a little blood. She wiped away the rest of the blood that had run down her neck unnoticed, leaving a red smear.

Hope they don't judge on appearance, she thought in an effort to cheer herself up. It didn't work but it was worth a try. She made it to the center of the circle with only her guard as companion in that empty space. She kept wondering why Bo wasn't allowed in the circle with her yet.

Her nerves were on edge as she stood there with so many eyes watching her. Sally felt stage fright might take over and make her run away. Holding on to the fear gave her the strength to stand her ground, not wanting to give the crowd something to feed off of. No point getting a riot going before the real fun started. Her eyes wandered frequently to where she had last seen Bo to help steady herself in this shifting tide of emotions.

A wavering in the air announced the use of magic before Sally felt it latch on to her body. The air about her rose in temperature as it pressed in. She knew the spell was one to hold her in place when her feet slid together and her elbows pressed inward to her body. With or without handcuffs, she would be immobilized by the sheer force of air that wrapped her now. This was a working used against the undead, lending credence to why a human guard stood by her instead of Bo.

Once the air settled down people started moving about and talking; they could rest easier now that the threat was bound. Bo entered the circle at a slow pace, each step deliberate. Standing next to her, he flashed a smile then turned to face the podium without a word.

All she could do was follow his lead and keep silent. The spell didn't allow anything else. Sweat dripped down her spine as she was forced to stand motionless; not even the gentle breeze blowing around them made it past the wards set upon her. Sally didn't know how much longer they would wait before the tribunal showed up, but she found when she tried to ask Bo her mouth wouldn't open. Panic started to rise up in her, and Bo must have felt it because he turned to her with sympathy in his eyes, his hand raised in a gesture to stay calm; then he was back to staring straight ahead again like a statue.

Drums beat in the distance, announcing the tribunal. Sally thought it a bit much for a lynching mob to be so formal when all they really wanted was her head on a platter. Bo had said in what little time they did have together that this had to be done in accordance with the laws set eons ago, or her head wouldn't be the only one to roll. It was the one thing he had been glad of; it gave them a fighting chance. No matter what happened next, she was glad to have him by her side.

But as each member of the tribunal entered the ambient glow of firelight one by one, her courage faltered. They wore deep red cloaks with amber scrolling insignia on the folded edging, hoods left unused. She could see by the waning light some were older than she thought they would be. Most of the undead seemed to get reborn between twenty to thirty years old, but a few of the tribunal actually had gray hair and a few more showed signs of wrinkling.

Sally was taken aback by the sight of such elder men and wondered if this might be cause for alarm or not. Might they have a different view on life, or was it a stigma given to anyone that showed deeper maturity? She wished she knew if it really mattered at all when the time came to place judgment. Fear swelled within her again as each of them took their place on either side of the podium.

Mathyas was the last to enter and stood directly behind the stand with head bowed, hood drawn over his head. His hands went out in an all-encompassing movement towards the center of the circle, sweeping in either direction until they were outstretched in the form of a scarecrow. Silence followed. Mathyas dropped his arms to his sides taking the last remaining steps to the podium before looking up at the quieted audience with approval.

"We have gathered tonight under the eyes of our gods to bear witness on the actions we take this night," he said with melodramatic flare, "to place judgment on one of our own. It saddens me to be among one of the chosen to make such a decision on someone else's life, but fate has brought us no other alternative. We must take into account the future of our race when making such drastic choices about another's life, or we become the animals the humans believe we are.

"Tonight is a turning point some of you are not aware of. We hope to be the guiding light in dark times ahead that have been foretold by many prophets over the centuries. This should bring us closer to a world where we won't have to hide in the forest but can be out in the open once more as we lived so long ago." He scanned the crowd for signs of doubt before continuing, "Let it be known for all that haven't been told, the lady before you is a Slaver. The first Slaver kept us locked away to do the humans' bidding until he was destroyed; he gave us reason to hide in the first place. We have looked to the stars, runes, and even old prophecy for clarity in what must be done tonight. We bare no ill will toward this young lady; we only wish to do what is right for our kind."

There were hushed murmurs rippling through the crowd; Sally was forced to hear some of them speak a little too loudly about being proud to witness the demise of such evil. Bo appeared to be heated by what was said around him, but most of all he focused his contempt straight at Mathyas. Sally watched as Bo never let his eyes wander too far from the speaker as he took in the surrounding member's expressions. She did the same and wished she hadn't. Heads bobbed up and down repeatedly to the words almost in cadence. The look on Bo's face only confirmed her newly surfaced fears. It seemed the odds of them getting out of this had diminished considerably.

Mathyas carried on for some time more, none of it in her favor, until she heard him ask Bo to speak. Bo took a step forward, looking at each of the members in turn.

"From what has been said so far, judgment is all but guaranteed before any case can be heard. The actions of a bygone age still haunt us today. Where is it truly written that this woman will take what was given to her and lash out in the same manner as the original Slaver did? Do you think what we do tonight might foster those kinds of feelings in her against our kind as her powers grow? Do not take lightly how each of you vote, as this will be the turning point Mathyas speaks so gravely about.

"I will do what I can to change your mind about how you feel towards Sally, the one standing before you awaiting your decision tonight, and hopefully enlighten you to who she is. Not what was told you by a throw of the dice," he finished on a somber note looking for some semblance of humanity among the tribunal but found none.

Sally lost concentration as a buzzing noise took over anything she could hear. No one else seemed to be aware of the incessant humming that plagued her now. As important as this trial was to her well-being, the words were lost to a hornet's nest in her ears. Bo appeared to be heated about something, but she couldn't make it out, and a tingling zipped up and down her body, distracting her more.

It was like someone had run bare electrical wire across her skin repeatedly, however lightly it first felt. The feeling intensified to an unbearable level, drawing unheard squeals from her mind. Sally imagined smoke tendrils rising from her skin as the pain grew worse, causing her to cringe with no way to escape the torment. She looked to the members of the tribunal for any glimmer of satisfaction.

No one even gave her a passing glance while Bo pleaded her case. She was drowning in her bloodless torment, on fire from the inside with no way to scream out. It came in dramatic pulses of horrific suffering, giving way to quick glimpses of what was happening, only to be washed away by the white heat of pain again. Tears ran down her cheeks as the only sign of anything going on when Bo turned to her in the middle of his speech, thinking those were tears thanking him for his effort. It was the last thing Sally saw as the whiteness of pure agony pressed away her sight. The waves of heat steadied to a constant burn, like she was being incinerated.

Through it all she continued to struggle against her entrapment, looking for a hole or some loose end to the spell that had been missed and finding that hole was more sense than sight. The pain drew too much in her, leaving little room for any other thought. She desperately wanted to scream, to let out the pent up energy from the unrelenting onslaught it brought.

The outreaches of her mind felt a rumbling shake from the ground in an earthquake fashion. She was sure she felt it the second time when the bonds holding her loosened a little. Now Sally was sure she was losing her mind.

Without so much as a warning she fell to the ground in a heap. She trembled in place, caught in an unstoppable seizure. The rumbling she first felt overrode her own and she sensed a presence over her as she vibrated on the dirt floor. Sound erupted so loud she closed her mouth, startled. When the noise stopped, Sally realized it was her own voice echoing out. She started up again, overjoyed that someone might hear her cries of pain.

A hand lightly touched her shoulder, but she bashed it away not knowing who had reached out for her. Still shaking, she managed to curl up into a ball, wailing out in anguish. When the sting of the imaginary cattle prods began to fade, so did her need to cry out. Sally laid there, tears cascading to the dirt floor. In the quiet of her weeping she heard no other sound.

Even the rumbling had ceased. In the silence a voice rang out, "Enough!"

Someone was intervening.

She knew that voice but couldn't place it. It was someone she had recently met, but her mind was still jumbled from the torment she'd just endured. No matter the source, it was a welcoming distraction. Sally's vision started to clear, and blurred sight gave way to forms and shapes of the tribunal in front of her. This was the last thing she wanted to see. She tried to roll away from the hateful sight of the tribunal but had no energy left.

Commotion ensued around her. Getting control of her emotions, Sally was able to whisper out for Bo through her raw throat. She was amazed he heard her at all when a hand settled on her shoulder again.

Awe escaped him, "We have company."

Bo asked, fearful she might pass out, "Are you OK to stand?"

She resisted the urge to be independent, and instead let him help her. Most of the action was facing away from the tribunal, making her all the more happy to look with the rest of the crowd. Past the deeper shadows of the forest, large forms emerged out of the blackness of night. More time had passed than she realized while being lobotomized by someone on the panel of judges. The first to emerge was Adelwin himself. Sally could see him because he stood taller than the rest.

Most bowed deeply as he passed, showing her what kind of respect his kind had in the camp. Looking past him she noticed larger, dark shapes following in his footsteps. He had gathered his clan to be present for her demise. Knowing she was doomed didn't dampen her relief at seeing another familiar face among the ruthless crowd. She followed Bo's lead and bowed as Adelwin approached them.

CHAPTER 28

"What is the meaning of this!" demanded Adelwin of the group.

Silence answered him back; no one stirred an inch from where they all stood. A deep grumbling came from the Neanderthal as Sally watched him meticulously scan the area, waiting for anyone to speak. His anger was reflected in the fire of the torches, which flared out of control. People standing close to the light scurried back from the raging fire it had become. Fear was evident in all their faces.

Mathyas finally spoke up after regaining his wits. "We have come together, O Great One, to convene on the judgment on a Slaver in our presence. You would remember well the last time one was allowed to roam free."

"You join together to connive and cheat this woman of her right to live, is what I see," Adelwin bellowed out with force. "You took no time to know this one as I did the first Slaver. He had a bad seed in him before the

Egyptians took hold of him. I will not say power corrupts, but in his case he chose to enslave our kind to further his own means."

Mathyas looked enraged but kept a civil tongue all the same. "You wish us to sit back and watch her as our people get taken one by one with her power?"

"And who is she going to enslave them for? We and everything around us are considered delusions of fantasy to the living, besides the Church. The Church does want her badly, and they have already hunted her. Do you find her that moronic, to work for the very ones chasing her down?" Adelwin's words burned with contempt for the Church as he waved his hands around angrily.

"We are only doing what is best for—"

"Stop your insistent babble! You think I cannot see what this truly is?"

Wind kicked up from all direction as Adelwin swept his arms out towards the waiting tribunal. Lightning cracked from the cloudless sky as the others in his party moved up to stand beside him, casting out magic as they went. Trees splintered from the thunderous force of the lightning strike. The Neanderthals formed a V-shape with Adelwin as the point and the rest facing outward to the cowering flock around them. They all stood with legs spread ready to pounce on the first that would think to move in their direction.

When Adelwin waved Sally over to him she was apprehensive to walk over with such a menacing group even if they were there to assist her. Adelwin looked back to Bo and gestured for him to do the same. When Bo was in place, Adelwin again placed his gaze back on the tribunal.

"I know many of you bought into the fear your leader convinced you of. I am here to tell you otherwise. This trial is over and Sally will go free." He made sure they all understood his words as he looked to each member for acknowledgement. All but Mathyas answered.

"She will not leave these lands unscathed. I cannot unleash such a being into the world with a clear conscience," he repeated with venomous intent.

"So be it," was all the Neanderthal said as he raised his hand.

At the same time his hand rose, so did Mathyas, rising a few feet off the ground. Adelwin spread his fingers, and the leader's limb spread accordingly like a marionette's doll on strings. Grunting spilled forth from Mathyas as he strained against unseen bonds not much different from Sally's own minutes before. Each movement of Adelwin's finger caused his extremities to tug away from his body, eliciting a screech of pain each time.

A flick of one finger pulled Mathyas's arm away from his body, leaving a trail of sinew stringing from his shoulder to what was left of the bicep. Mathyas's screams of pain rang out into the night as the limb fell to the ground. Blood spewed out from fresh wounds onto some of the tribunal still standing too close. Each finger that flicked out removed another limb.

Cries for mercy were met unanswered. "You bound and tormented Sally until we appeared. You beg for mercy when there was none offered to her." Adelwin peered down at her briefly before setting to work again.

The last was the head, and when the Neanderthal moved his thumb a sickening pop sounded as the bones pulled away silencing the screaming leader once and for all and giving way to a limbless torso floating in the air.

Adelwin dropped his hand to release what was left of the body. Screeching wails still rang in the air, gone unnoticed until Sally realized they came from her. She quieted down when a hand lit softly to her shoulder. Bo stood facing her, trying to talk her down from the panic attack she was in. Sally was in such a state of hysterics she didn't think anyone could calm her down. However, the sight of Bo and his soft words brought her back from the brink.

She fell into him with her hands held up to the crook of his neck remembering at the last moment she still wore the handcuffs. It didn't matter to her they were still on, so long as there was someone to hold her at that moment. She needed the feel of another body right now to be connected to this world.

"I can take care of those for you," Adelwin said.

Without him touching her or the cuffs, they unlocked and floated from her to the ground a few yards away. The release of the gold filled her with the familiar power she had come to know and love. Her control over the flood was better, but it still knocked her knees out from under her. The magic washing away her pain still lingering from the trial. Bo held her close as she regained her balance and thanked him for holding her before she passed out.

CHAPTER 29

Sally awoke on a picnic bench staring up at the stars. She had trouble remembering where she was or how she had got there. It all came back to her when Bo leaned over to check on her. Sally looked back and smiled sheepishly at his grin before pushing herself up to a sitting position.

Pacing not too far away was Adelwin with his hands crossed behind his back, one hand clutching the other. He seemed worried until he saw her get up, and then he came to her in a blurring movement. Sally could not tell if it was her head swaying from the episode she had or if he really moved that fast. In any case she was glad to have him sit next to her.

"The ward I placed on you during our first meeting was set off by the handcuffs," he explained in a rush. "I had feared something like this would happen and put what protection I thought might help on you."

"Then the enormous blast from the handcuffs being put on didn't come from me?" She shook her head at the thought of remembering it. "I think that might have spurred the crowd into the frenzy they were in. I can see where the connection to me being such a threat might come from with that kind of power."

Adelwin looked up at her somberly. "I did it when we shook hands. It was the closest place I thought gold would touch your skin, and I was right, although I sometimes forget how strong I can be when magic is done hastily."

She couldn't help but laugh. "You forgot something you've been doing for eons? Hard to believe."

He bellowed back with his own deep laughter. "We Elders refrain from using too much magic. Most of the time we just wander around the forests until a hunter spots us. We use our magic only when forced or in self-defense. Can't let the hunters catch up to us, or there might be more than blurry photos."

The thought of all the old shows and new ones still being made about the abominable snowman and Sasquatch with their blurred photos and poor camera footage made her giggle. To think this Elder was one of the furry so-called sightings. Truth is stranger than fiction sometimes.

Sally twitched at the thought but felt she needed to know. "I really don't want to change the subject, but why did you tear Mathyas to shreds?"

Adelwin sat scratching his head for a while. "It's not that I wanted to bring on his demise. Mathyas would have done far worse to you or anyone else, for that matter, if he was left alive. He was set to see your body pulled apart just like his was. We rarely intervene with any tribunal decisions, but in your case it was more than necessary. The future is never as clear you might think you see it, which is why one of my fellow Elders is speaking with Zemra right now."

Bo shook his head when Sally turned to ask who that was. She had time now to find out some of the finer details later. "So, no time-outs given to the undead?" she asked. "And I suppose his head didn't ramble on after it was removed because of a spell."

Bo took this one. "We talked about that before, the graveyards. He will be kept separated, with each part of him buried in a different cemetery for safekeeping. The Elders will be the only ones to call for his resurrection when they think his penance is over. A trusted man of mine, Michal, is overseeing the whole thing. A good man he is to make the trek to all those locations." Speaking before he thought it out, Bo said, "The idiot's head needed to stay quiet. I for one didn't want to hear it rattle on and on."

Snickering came from an unlikely source, Adelwin.

"OK, time for the big question," Sally said. "What of me? I know this trial thing is done and over now, but I'm sure there's at least a little animosity aimed in my direction." She was unsure if she wanted to hear the answer.

Adelwin could only smile at her directness, "Only time can heal all wounds, and that is something you're not going to run out of. As for this camp? While you were out we had to make compromises to assure the people you could do no harm to them. No matter how old you get, self-preservation never dies.

"You leaving in the morning and never coming back—that was the only agreement the remaining tribunal would consider," Bo said as he looked out at the groups of undead milling about, keeping what they thought was a safe distance from the new Slaver. "The Elders offered to ward the current boarders with a special zap for you if you ever got close. Sorry to tell you but they didn't want to take chances later."

Sally bobbed her head in agreement. "Don't blame them. Although I can't see myself ever wanting to come back either."

Adelwin shook his finger at her. "I promised to take the time to teach you what cannot be taught by any other. How could I hold up to that if you could not enter these mountains again? I made their fears work against them when they asked to bar you from the mountains—and they got a prison. They won't leave the boundaries now in fear you might be waiting for one of them."

They had a good laugh about it, and then Adelwin proclaimed that she needed rest for the morning hike down the mountain. He had one more detail to share that couldn't be ignored, "Because of the compromise you can't be seen in these woods for a year and I won't leave my home just to teach. Don't give up hope, by then the camp should be back to normal and you'll have a less likely chance of harassment."

Sally looked up with a bit of sadness for such a new friendship to be placed on hold because of others. She nodded her head solemnly, speaking in hushed tones, "I will return on the hour when this year passes to learn. I promise."

He bid farewell and walked them to Sally's cabin beneath an overbearing group of trees. He placed a ward around the cabin that was tuned to either Bo or herself to pass. He explained the boundary ward would work the same way, except the Elders would give Bo the location for safe passage over the new boundary. After they crossed, it would sense her passing and close up tight on its own. From there Bo would have to guide her to the dirt road. He wished Sally good luck and to see her soon as he walked away.

From all that had happened, Sally was too amped up to sit, let alone lie down. She began to pace the room before Bo could stop her.

"It's the adrenaline rush that's hitting now," he said. "Knowing you're not going to die anymore has your endorphins running at full tilt, but you have to sit and relax before this all crashes down on you."

All she could do was listen to his advice. He had not been wrong yet. All she wanted to do was expend some pent-up energy, to feel the release that always brought on a good night's sleep. She tried to entice Bo into lying on the bed with her, but as always he refused. The part of her that still lived called out for him to touch her again like they had before she passed out. To caress her in his arms one more time, holding her near him in a deep embrace.

He looked flustered at the way she was acting before storming out with a quick good night. She bit the pillow and screamed into it as loud as she could, banging her free hand against the mattress. Frustration overrode her compulsion to need him anymore. The night would be just as well without him...why did she still think about this man that way?

He had done nothing to bring it on, but she was so drawn to him it made no sense. The way he acted gave her some inkling he had his own pent-up feeling for her as well. Bo had said that part of him was long dead, and yet he tried to ignore what he felt for her. Only time would tell, and Adelwin said they had nothing but time.

As those thoughts swam through her mind, she drifted into sleep before she knew it.

**

The sun shone brightly past the thin white drapes hung over the window, waking Sally from the fitful dreams she'd had all night about her trial. The dreadful feeling of being electrified over and over kept her from reaching any form of real sleep all night. Even awake, the ghostly feeling still ran along her skin. Unable to shake the foreboding aftereffects, she got up to peek past the curtains. Motion around the camp was pretty much the same as its northern companion, just another place filled with people that never slept.

Sally made her way outside to search out Bo and apologize for her motives the night before. It's not like she hadn't tried something like this before, but that was when she could not control the urges from the magical overload. Last night had been all her, and Bo must have known it to storm out like that. She had to make it up to him somehow.

She ran into him by accident as he was bringing her a plate of food and she was occupied looking the opposite way. They almost collided if not for Bo's fast feet moving him out of striking distance. She said sorry and thank you for the food all in the same breath.

He pointed to a nearby bench and she followed him to it. Once she was finished eating, they would have to be on their way out of camp soon or face the consequences of the arrangement the Elders had made. She had not asked and did not want to know what those consequences were, so she ate with haste. Unlike the other camp, this one held no good-byes to say, just the feeling of good riddance.

Bo collected their few things, handing Sally hers to carry, and made their way through camp to the place the Elders had prepared for her exit. They slowly walked two miles, mostly in silence, before crossing a hiking trail that would lead her to the road ahead. Sally felt bad they were going to part on such a sour note. She could not keep herself from apologizing again.

"I can't explain what happened last night, but I won't deny it either." Her hands searched for her pockets for something to do while she waited for him to respond.

When he didn't, she prodded him to walk her until they could see the road before letting him off the hook. It was another mile before he said anything at all, and she refused to fill the gap with unnecessary chatter. What men would do to keep from speaking made no sense to her.

Bo stumbled a few times before getting the words out in a sentence: "It has been a long time since I had any feeling for another. When you live as long as we do, the turmoil a lasting relationship can cause might be worse than anything you've had to endure in your past life. This isn't something to take lightly, and I sure as hell won't be dragged through the mud again."

Sally replied, "I get it, I do. Waiting is something I'm used to anyway. When we meet up again, I might see your point of view and keep up the friendship; however, if I don't change my mind then you'll have to make do with a groupie following you around, deal?"

"Deal."

The road was in sight too soon for Sally. She had hoped for a little more time with Bo before saying goodbye, wondering when they would next meet up. He offered only a quick hug, and she took it like a hungry child to a full bottle of milk. It was three hundred yards to the road, and Bo promised to not leave until she made it there. She used the walk to go over some of the things he had told her while she ate breakfast. He had given her directions to the nearest depot for the undead, a place called the ghost train. Just like the supernatural to use spooky names. When she asked what it was, he would only say she had to see it. Other contacts would be given to her from there so anything written down would not be lost. She turned to wave as the road was almost under her feet, giving him the sign so he could head back to camp.

**

She's on her way. Bo struggled with the thought. He should be down there with her to show her the ropes a little longer, but there were a few more things to do back at camp before he could follow. She would get along fine if someone wanted to rough her up; that wasn't what worried him. The Church was still out there even if they stopped the search for her so soon. Apparently they had lost the trail thanks to Adelwin and headed back to their home base. Sally would have safe passage to the ghost train and from there he could find her.

Bo watched her wave back to him letting him know he didn't have to stand around anymore. He headed back the way they had come, following the trail in a half dream state. She had really screwed with his brain last night and the thought of her made him turn back one last time to see her swatting at the air and dodging around by the edge of the road. *Kind of cold out for mosquitoes*, He thought. Bo could only think there must have been a car coming for her to hang around so long by the roadside.

When he stopped moving there was were quiet reports of a gun with a silencer. The repeated thudding sound from the silencer made it clear why Sally just stood there now; she was being shot at with tranquilizer darts. Before he could react a van pulled up, and two men jumped out to scoop her inside.

Bo ran as fast as he could but refrained from doing anything mystical in the light of day because if someone saw him do magic then he would have more problems with the Elders. When he made it to the road the van was gone. In the distance he heard another car approaching with the music blaring. The song fit his mood as the band Hurt sang out "Wars." All he could do was stand there and say, "Shit!"

ABOUT THE AUTHOR

Adam Santo was born and raised in Southern California before joining the Army for his short lived career as a soldier. The Army stationed him in Colorado when he realized this to be the most beautiful place earth to him. Currently living in Florida, Adam knows he will one day return to Colorado.

Made in the USA
Charleston, SC
13 March 2011